THAT NEVER DIES

TERESA RYAN

Copyright © 2017 Teresa Ryan
All rights reserved
First Edition

PAGE PUBLISHING, INC.
New York, NY

First originally published by Page Publishing, Inc. 2017

ISBN 978-1-63568-855-9 (Paperback)
ISBN 978-1-63568-856-6 (Digital)

Printed in the United States of America

CHAPTER 1

Not even Fiona Morgan's supersensitive natural psychic powers had prepared her for this turn of events in her life. The year was 1959. Here she was in this rundown abandoned castle reeking of dampness, lugging her suitcase under the tall stone archway of Bedford Castle in County Tipperary in Ireland. Fiona had no one to turn to for advice in this hopeless dilemma. Imagine the audacity of the mayor of Limerick, Rory McCormack, believing she would marry him. At five feet six inches tall, weighing 120 pounds with corn silk–blonde hair framing an exquisitely sensitive face and eyes of an unfathomable sorrow, Fiona was a poor match for the three-hundred-pound brawny man. His arms looked as if they belonged to a boxer. But it was the coldness and narrowness of his steel-grey eyes that terrified her. The determined chin bespoke a man not to be crossed.

Fiona had never entertained the idea of marriage. At eighteen years of age, it was far from her mind.

The clock of Bedford belfry tolled nine at night. Fiona thought she was alone, when a sobbing voice interrupted her. Was she losing her senses? she wondered. She stiffened, every nerve and sinew on edge. So it was true, she thought, that most of these castles were haunted. The sobbing continued, forcing her to drop her suitcase immediately. If need be, she would leave it behind and run as fast as her legs would carry her.

Fiona went through a long narrow corridor with wayward branches brushing against octagonal stained-glass windows, eyes wide with terror. Her footsteps echoed through the stone battlements.

Arriving at a huge chapel, she forced the door open. It made creaking noises. Yet the man who knelt at the prie-dieu did not turn his head. His thick mop of shiny back hair was unruly. His shoulders were broad. Perhaps he had not heard Fiona. Should she flee or interrupt his sobbing? She did not want to approach a stranger in this frame of mind.

It seemed an eternity before he turned around. His face was filled with pain, joy, and an unspeakable sorrow. Although tears brimmed in his liquid brown eyes, it seemed to make him very appealing, not at all detracting from a ruggedly handsome face. Unbidden, tears streamed down the man's aristocratic face as he turned his head sideways in an attempt to conceal his grief.

"Yes," he said, brown eyes dark and angry.

Haltingly, she said, "Can I help you?" her voice choking with emotion.

"I don't think so." He snapped out a white silk handkerchief.

"Why are you so distressed, if I may venture to ask?"

There was a pause before he resumed, "My beautiful wife . . . died. She is buried . . . here." He turned to a vault in the center of the chapel behind him. His hand seemed to caress the vault as he stroked it and allowed it to remain there for some minutes.

"I'm terribly sorry to hear that."

"I quite understand."

"Thank you, but it only concerns me."

"Do you?" There was a hint of hardness of his mouth.

To her surprise, she was not annoyed.

"Only a person," he continued, "who has been through this can fully comprehend what it is to love so deeply and to have her snatched away by the jaws of death."

"Are you blind?" She looked at him quizzically, aware of the long cane beside him.

"Yes. I hope you never know what it's like to be blind. Maybe and that's a big question mark. There's an advantage to being blind. My other senses, particularly for music, have been heightened. I never appreciated music to such a degree till this blindness struck."

"You mean you weren't always blind?"

"No. This struck me like lightning on the day of the funeral."

"Maybe it's just a passing phase."

"Nonsense. I can't see. It'll take a miracle to restore my sight."

"If you became blind so suddenly, surely sight can return just as suddenly."

"That's what the doctors say. They could find no organic disease. I hope they're right. Ophthalmology consultants diagnosed it as psychic blindness. The medical terminology for it is visual agnosia. It occurs one in two billion cases. They claim I was unable to face the reality of the death of my wife."

"Had she been sick . . . a long . . . time?"

"That's the awful part." His face brightened, and his eyes glowed with happiness. There was not a trace of the empty vacant eyes of a blind man. He resumed, "She was as healthy as I am. Never sick a day in her life. She was standing, talking to me. She dropped to the floor, dead."

"What a dreadful shock."

"She had an embolism, which journeyed to her heart. She was gone in a matter of minutes."

"Say no more."

"I don't want to burden you with my troubles." There was a kindly quality to his voice. "You're far too young and pretty to be burdened with such matters."

"Thank you."

"We were only married two years."

"You must have been very much in love with her."

"She was my joy, my life, my treasure. I'd never known I could be so happy."

"That's certainly a tragedy. God does not give us more than we can bear in life."

"I wonder. Often I feel this is unbearable. I'm a nuisance, telling you my troubles."

"Not at all. I only wish there was something I could do for you."

"Forgive my seeming rudeness when you spoke. I didn't mean it. Lately I've been lashing out without provocation."

"I'm sure you mean well."

"It's just that I come here at night when the loneliness seems unbearable. I think of my wife lying here alone in this cold, lonely castle, never to see her face again, never to hear her melodious voice. She was beautiful, sweet, and we were totally in love."

"It must have been wonderful to have experienced such depths of love."

"When you find love, cherish it, because it may never pass your way again. I know there can never be another love like Christiana."

"Time heals all wounds."

"I wish I could believe that now . . ."

"I'll say a little prayer for you."

"Do that. I shall be very grateful to you."

He was silent for a few minutes. Fiona felt very uncomfortable, not knowing whether to go or stay.

He said, "Enough about me. I'm Robert Von Pragh."

"And I'm Fiona Morgan."

Robert extended his hand and shook hers warmly. He nestled her slender hand within both of his. Then he covered her hands possessively. The warmth of his personal contact sent shivers of joy up her arms till they embraced her whole body. It seemed as if a seraphic light was beaming through her.

Never before had Fiona felt such bliss. Hastily she withdrew her hand and turned her head to the side. She thought it silly to do so, when in reality, Robert could not see her. Yet his gaze was so piercing that it was difficult to believe he could not see her. An owl hooted in some corner of Bedford Castle.

"Please don't be afraid," Robert said.

"I'm not," Fiona lied.

"There's no reason whatsoever. You're here very late." He looked into her dazzling green eyes.

In Robert's eyes, Fiona detected compassion and kindness of the highest quality. Of course, she was wrong to misjudge him, she thought.

"I come here at night," Robert said, "to be alone with my wife. Usually there's no intrusion by strangers. The porter has gone for the night. He knows better than to disturb me here in the chapel."

"I'm sure you're beloved wife is with angels and at peace in heaven."

"Strange though it may seem, I never thought about that."

"In heaven there is no suffering. Moreover, she's not alone."

"Are you insinuating that I should be comforted by that thought?"

"Death, as we mortals know, is merely a transition to the spirit world. No sadness prevails there. We'll all join the spirit world one day."

"The sooner my time comes, the better off I'll be." He looked heavenward with a faraway look in his eyes.

"You must not harbor such thoughts. I'm sure your wife would want you to carry on in life and be happy."

"Christiana always only wanted the best for me. Like most men, I was often selfish. How I would do anything now to please her when it's too late."

"It's not too late to go forward in life. By helping and being kind to others, you may bring a semblance of happiness to yourself. Your sight may even be restored if you ask Christiana."

"For one so young"—he appraised her in a pleasing manner—"you seem very philosophical."

"Am I? I never thought so."

"Life must have shouldered you with its share of burdens."

Fiona swallowed hard, knowing that what he said was true and never more appropriate than now. She felt like bursting into tears.

"I sense you're upset," Robert said.

"I've very few worries compared to you."

"You're referring to my blindness, no doubt."

"Yes."

"Don't let that worry your pretty head. When I go to church now, I feel transported to another world. My senses are heightened to such a degree that I can hardly describe. All my senses except of course for my sight."

"I love music more than anything else. One day I hope to be an opera singer."

"That takes a lot of practice."

"I've been practicing since the age of seven."

"I wish you the very best of luck. But the longer you live, the more you get beaten down in life. Nowhere more so than in the arts."

"I'm prepared to face that challenge."

"Now tell me what's bothering you, but only if you feel like it."

"Don't worry about me," she said with a peremptory wave of the hand.

"You baffle me. You also worry me. What brings a frail young slip of a lady like yourself here alone on the night of the full moon with nothing but a handbag?"

Fiona was dumbstruck. She imagined Robert must be preoccupied with his own troubles. Yet she faltered at the idea of telling him she had a suitcase and nowhere to stay for the night.

The wind whispered and whistled through chinks and doorways of Bedford Castle, causing Fiona to shudder. She must not reveal her dilemma. God knows what Robert would think. Maybe he would take advantage of her. Almost instantly she banished that idea from her mind. How preposterous to entertain such a notion.

Fiona could hardly believe her good fortune sitting next to Lord Robert. She felt a mixture of momentary panic and dizzying exhilaration. His mere presence caused shivers of delight to course through her being. Instinctively, she knew this should not be. Yet she was incapable of controlling such tumultuous feelings.

CHAPTER 2

Fiona stretched out on the cold stone floor with an Irish fisherman's sweater underneath her. She wore another sweater on her body and threw the coat over her. She detected a faint pleasing manly odor from the cushion. It was as if Robert had been in the fields all day among pine trees.

Fiona pressed her head into the cushion, in despair at the whole confusing situation that lay ahead of her. If Rory McCormack came here right now, Robert would never hear her behind the heavy door if she cried out. Perhaps he would be too engrossed with his wife that he would be literally oblivious to outside influences. Fiona admonished herself for being so pessimistic. She must not put herself in the same situation as Robert to think that life was futile.

Suddenly the "Hallelujah" chorus spun around in her head. She could hear the uplifting strains, which transported her to a higher plane. Ever since childhood, Fiona had loved to sing opera and Gregorian chant. She knew of no other friends who liked opera. But that had not deterred her. In fact, it had spurred her on to know more and more so that she had a huge collection in her home.

Silently it was Fiona's life ambition to appear at an opera house of high repute and to pour her heart and soul into an opera. Many a time she practiced in front of the full-length mirror and visualized an audience sitting in front of her. There would be no reason for stage fright, she reasoned.

Fiona would get lost in her music and think of the painstaking hours the composer had written and rewritten his music. Opera lifted her to a higher spirit realm that she could not explain. Deep in her heart she vowed no Rory McCormack would force her to marry him and lead a boring life. It had never been her life's ambition. At six years of age, she had a vision where she saw herself singing to tumultuous applause. Had that vision been the imaginings of a lonely child who desperately needed her mother?

Fiona had been philosophical about the absence of her parents since birth. Even though many a time she cried herself to sleep and wondered how her parents could leave her alone in the world, she realized she was fortunate to have plenty to eat.

Occasionally, Fiona had rebelled against the strict boarding school upbringing by the Ursuline nuns. She knew they were preparing her for a life on her own. One time she heard two nuns whisper about the unfortunate girl Fiona Morgan, and wondered what it meant. Because she should not have been eavesdropping, she did not dare ask them to elaborate on their statement.

Fiona only knew that boarding school was paid for, and not by the nanny with whom she had lived. Although the nanny, Mary, was kind, she always remained cold and aloof. She constantly reminded Fiona that she was not her mother.

When Fiona had asked who her mother was, she merely had said, "I do not know. I've heard she's a good person, and that's all."

But Fiona had retorted, "If she's good, I must be bad, because she doesn't come to see me."

"There may be other reasons that we don't know, Fiona. I'm sure when you're father gets better, you'll see him."

"Oh! I can't wait," Fiona had said.

At four years of age, Fiona recalled with great fondness the time her father had come to see her. Even though he seemed very old and was constantly wheezing and coughing, he would play with her. He had brought a bagful of toys, and she could see the love in his eyes as he watched her playing.

Fiona had remembered the gnarled old hands as the two of them had walked along the lonely country road parallel to a forest. Fiona had felt proud of her father and had felt loved and cosseted by him. She was well aware too of the cottagers and small shopkeepers peeping from half doors and windows to have a glimpse of her father. They seemed to look at him with a mixture of love and pity.

"Fiona, my dear," she had recalled him saying, "when I'm gone, always remember that I loved you more than life itself. You'll hear many stories about me, but you are like a breath of spring."

How Fiona's eyes had lit up and how ecstatic she had felt. Deep down she knew he had meant it. There were times when her father had to pause for breath, fumble for a spray that he had kept in his tweed jacket, and with faltering hands, spray two puffs of the inhaler contents into his mouth. Miraculously, his breathing would improve, and she would skip along by his side.

The second time Fiona had seen her father, he appeared to have grown very old and weary looking. Somehow Fiona had sensed that she would never see him again. He had crushed Fiona to him, and tears had streamed down her cheeks. Her love for him was overwhelming. A sense of desolation and despair had enveloped her when the pilot of her father's aeroplane had helped him up the steps.

A heavy burden seemed to weigh Fiona down as she had watched her father wave, and the plane took off for Virginia in the United States. How far, far away the country had seemed.

The clock in the belfry tolled ten. Sounds within and without frightened Fiona. Cold and alone, she imagined sleep would be impossible. Her psychic powers were at their best tonight, something she attributed to the full moon hovering in the sky. And when she was in such a psychic state, she was receptive to everything around her and felt astonishingly aware of her powers. She could communicate with the departed, those about to depart this earthly world, the sick, and those about to get married.

Fiona closed her eyes wearily. Bedford Castle reeked of dampness, and Fiona hoped she would not catch a cold. She breathed deeply in and out in an attempt to relax. She began to meditate and prayed her guardian angel would keep her safe.

It was preposterous to think that she would sleep in Bedford Castle. What would sustain her through the hours of gloom and darkness? Fiona tossed and turned on the cold stone floor. Gradually she became more relaxed. While she was in a trance, the castle became pitch-black. Fiona's heart skipped a beat. She was deathly afraid.

Suddenly from the corner of the darkness emanated a white blur transforming itself into a brilliant opalescent light in the shape of a star. The light increased in intensity, yet it did not hurt Fiona's eyes. From the center of the light materialized a tall, elegant lady clad in a full-length white diaphanous gown. She moved with a grace and elegance that belied her years. In actual fact, Fiona could not determine her age.

The apparition moved slowly and gently towards Fiona. Unexpectedly, she halted in her track. She said, "I hope I haven't frightened you, Fiona."

"Oh No!" replied Fiona spontaneously, surprised at her response. Fiona became less nervous.

Then the apparition said, "This is your grandmother, Fiona. We never met in life, but I've always watched out for you from the spirit world."

Fiona wanted to hear everything the apparition had to say. She listened intently.

The voice, soft and melodious, said, "Do not be afraid. I hope I haven't frightened you."

While there was no physical contact, Fiona felt the presence of a reassuring hand on her right shoulder. A pause ensued.

With grim foreboding, the voice said, "Evil surrounds you. Evil lurks in this town for you." The apparition continued, "You must leave Ireland. It's an unlucky country for you. You must flee to London. There, you will meet fame and fortune and true love." She smiled a beatific smile.

Then the apparition disappeared into a mist. Fiona wanted to cry out and ask her spirit grandmother to return. There had been so many unanswered questions about Fiona's family. Nobody would be able to give her all the details better than her grandmother.

Even to Fiona, her mother and grandparents were a complete mystery. Why the mystery? Why had Fiona never met her mother? As she had been born in the United States, what was her mother's nationality? Was it possible she had died at birth? Maybe the subject was too painful for her father to discuss.

But it was excruciatingly painful for Fiona. It was also an embarrassment. Sometimes she felt the children at boarding school whispered behind closed doors about the unusual circumstances of Fiona. Fortunately, probing and causing embarrassment were not tolerated by the Ursuline nuns.

Impeccable manners, social graces, and decent conduct were an integral part of boarding school behavior. Sometimes Fiona imagined that her father's wealth played a part in her presence at this exclusive boarding school. Her father had no tolerance for lazy people. Despite the fact that his manner was gruff, to say the least, Fiona adored him.

Impossible though it was to contact her spirit grandmother, Fiona was sure that one day she would find answers, which heretofore were not forthcoming. Yet Fiona's spirit grandmother's brief appearance had wrought a peace and tranquility within her that previously had eluded her. With her grandmother's mission accomplished, Fiona would not have such an experience again from the other side.

Surprisingly, Fiona awakened not one bit afraid. She felt secure in the knowledge that somebody was taking care of her. Fiona felt a rising tide of confidence that she would be able to tackle whatever lay ahead.

CHAPTER 3

Fiona awakened to the crowing of a cock in some distant farmyard. She felt revitalized after a good night's sleep. Was it perhaps, as she believed, due to the visit of her spirit grandmother? Or was it the reassuring presence of Lord Von Pragh?

The sun shone fitfully through steel barred windows of the castle. As leaves drifted into the castle and whirled and danced round on the floor, Fiona awaited eagerly for the appearance of Lord Von Pragh. She would have loved to see that anguished aristocratic face in repose, sleeping near the vault, free of care and worry.

Fiona realized that it was absolutely out of the question for her to knock on the heavy metal door. It was Lord Von Pragh's private chapel to be shared only with his deceased wife. What good it did him was a total mystery to Fiona. As these thoughts whirred round in her head, she was fully clothed and on her feet. She imagined she heard a stirring behind her. It wasn't a figment of her imagination.

When Fiona turned round, Lord Von Pragh greeted her warmly. "Good morning," he said, and his tone was cheerful. His smile warmed the cockles of her heart.

"I hope you slept well," she said.

"I did indeed. Usually I do not."

"I slept quite well too."

"The floor must have been quite uncomfortable."

"I was so tired that it didn't matter. Of course, it was nervous exhaustion more than anything else."

"What are you going to do today?" he enquired.

"My mind is made up. I'm leaving for England."

"England? Here I thought I'd met a nice, special friend."

"You've made a friend. I feel I should leave Ireland under present circumstances. By the time the mayor of Limerick finds out, he'll have forgotten me, I hope."

"You can always count on me for help. Remember that. Will you, Fiona?" He looked eye to eye straight at her.

Although Robert's gaze made her feel somewhat uncomfortable, she instinctively knew he was sincere. Was it sorrow, she wondered, that had made him empathetic to his fellow human beings? Was it because he needed a friend every bit as much as she did? Was it that his dysfunctional blindness made him more aware of the feelings of others?

Suddenly Fiona realized how lucky she was compared to Lord Robert. Yes, he may have all the trappings of worldly success, but it availed him nothing when he was not able to see.

"When my gardener comes," Lord Robert said, "I'll fetch the chauffeur to drive us to your destination. By the way, where are you going?"

"To Dublin."

"A bit of a trip for me. It's a while since I've been there. It'll be nice going with you."

Sparks of delight lit up Fiona's eyes at the prospect. In a way, she was glad Robert could not see her enthusiasm. Or could he? she wondered. She knew that a man beset with psychic blindness could not see as long as he believed it. All Fiona knew was that in a matter of hours, she would not see Robert again. Already she was beginning to miss him. She regarded him as her protector in this cold, cruel, and unfeeling world. She questioned whether he felt as much alone in the world as she did.

Fiona thought it strange that considering she had lived in this town for the last eighteen years, she had not heard of Lord Robert. Miraculously, he had come into her social sphere as she was about to embark on a new life with new friends and in a different country. Yet she remembered her spirit grandmother's advice, and she was not about to contradict or misinterpret the message she had delivered.

If Ireland was an unlucky place for Fiona, she must seek a different country to live. From what she had read in magazines and newspapers, England was cosmopolitan with different nationalities living and working side by side.

Fiona would not have to worry about the mayor of Limerick with power and influence who was capable of thwarting her at every twist and turn. It seemed that this man had underestimated the strong willpower of Fiona.

Opera singing was Fiona's first love. It took a situation like this to determine her course in life. She asked herself why on earth she would entertain the notion of marriage before she had learned to live and support herself.

In her mind's eye, Fiona worried about money. She would have to watch every penny she spent and must not spend foolishly. Only necessities must be considered by her. How Fiona wished that she had a few hundred pounds at her disposal.

Even though Fiona was the only daughter of a tobacco multi-millionaire and was entitled to a trust fund, she would not be able to receive it. Her account was in trust by lawyers of the bank. The bank forwarded the check to Fiona on the first of each month. But because her surrogate mother had been somehow indebted to the lord mayor of Limerick, she would be afraid not to reveal Fiona's whereabouts.

Fiona recalled one cold wintry night while she was stoking the coals in the fireplace and her surrogate mother was in a talkative mood. Fiona had piped up and said, "Why did you not marry?"

Reluctantly, her surrogate mother had told her of her longstanding relationship with the mayor. She had said she would be eternally indebted to him. She recalled the year her brother had killed another patron of the local tavern in a drunken brawl. She had related how, through the influences of the mayor, her brother who would have faced several years, if not a lifetime, in prison for the murder he had been acquitted.

"The mayor had used me," she had said with a twinge of bitterness. "It was a question of he's flesh of my flesh and blood of my blood. Was I going to live a life of shame in front of my neighbors while my brother rotted away in prison?"

Fiona's surrogate mother further explained that she had been in love with the mayor even though there were many traits about him that were less than admirable. He was a manipulative politician who used his cunning to sway people including her.

Thus, Fiona felt that her surrogate mother would probably always be indebted to the mayor. Was it not only natural that the mayor would use his influence to make her brother happy and force Fiona to marry him?

CHAPTER 4

While Fiona tidied up her scant belongings on Bedford Castle floor, Robert retreated to the chapel. The quiet from within and without was interrupted by male voices. The gardener and the chauffeur entered the banquet hall. Fiona felt very embarrassed at their glances towards her. Then she thought it was probably her imagination that was active and she was overwrought. The chauffeur knocked on the chapel door and opened it.

Lord Robert said, "Ms. Morgan and I shall be leaving for Dublin as soon as possible."

"Today is fair day, Your Lordship," the chauffeur said.

"Of course. That means we must make haste. The livestock take over the streets today."

"Yes, sir."

Fiona was positively thrilled at the prospect of going to Dublin in the company of Lord Robert Von Pragh. Momentarily, a pang of guilt stabbed at her heart at the prospect she would be parting with him in Dublin.

How was a blind man torn by unresolved guilt and handicapped by blindness going to manage on his own? she wondered. She wanted to console him, to comfort him, to be by his side when he needed her. Probably he would bark and snap at her. But this she must forgive. She allowed for the fact that more than likely this was not his true nature. If it were, why should he mourn so long a time for the death of his wife? Only a man who had experienced great joy could live in such depth of sorrow, she reasoned.

Fiona could change her mind, but the risk was too enormous. Yet now circumstances could be different. Fiona would have Lord

Robert to protect her. Without a shadow of a doubt, he would be her fortress in time of challenge and despair. Yet his mind was totally focused on his dead wife. Neither woman nor mortal would be able to sever them if death had not succeeded. Fiona was still convinced that death was the final parting between the living and people in the spirit realm.

Could it be that Christiana from the spirit world influenced Lord Von Pragh's every action? A daunting presumption on Fiona's part, yet nevertheless one that could exist. Fiona had recalled the local folklore where the dead had risen from the grave to warn a loved one of impending danger. Was Fiona a present threat or danger to a dead wife? Time would tell. For now, it seemed impossible.

Yet the characteristic cold, aloof demeanor of Lord Von Pragh meant two distinct possibilities. Either he was afraid of releasing his own natural emotions or he had not gotten over the grieving process of Christiana. Two years?

Was it within the bounds of normalcy, or did it indicate a more disturbing influence in the life of Lord Von Pragh? And the disturbing menace could only be Fiona. She who desperately needed help in her present predicament by a male who could fight man to man for Fiona. His absence could leave her prey to the depravities any single woman could face.

As much as Fiona wanted to be in Lord Robert's life, she felt Lord Robert had no such intention. Since she hardly knew him, she must not consider that he would be significant in her life.

The driver announced that the car was at their disposal. He opened the door while Fiona sat in the backseat. Lord Robert followed. The door was closed.

The driver positioned himself behind the wheel of the Daimler, and they were off. Fiona wished she could marry Lord Von Pragh.

CHAPTER 5

Suddenly the car started increasing in speed on down the leafy pathway under trees shedding their summer mantle. It moved on slowly down a narrow street where pigs squealed in a pen. The driver braked instantly to avoid an accident. Her face brushed briefly against his, increasing the tumult from within. Nevertheless, he put his hand forward to prevent her from falling off the seat.

Fiona sensed Lord Robert's cold, formal reserve that she knew must be maintained by him. He was a strikingly handsome man, with the morning sun glinting on his hair, which was parted jauntily on the left side. Was he perhaps avoiding being close to someone so that he would not fall in love again? Was it the spirit of his wife intervening so that he could not love another woman? The thought made her blood run cold.

Was Fiona running ahead of herself? The mere fact that he had decided to go to Dublin with her was no indication of love. Maybe he had business there, and now was as good a time as any to do so. He would kill two birds with one stone.

"I feel relaxed in your company, Fiona," Lord Robert said.

"I'm delighted to hear that," she replied.

"It's quite unusual for me. After Christiana died, many eligible women were introduced to me to help me forget her. I couldn't. I can't now. I don't think I ever will. My only solace was in playing the piano."

"I'm sure your friends meant well."

"I've no doubt about that. But this prolonged grief has caused many of them to withdraw. They seemed to grow tired of hearing me talking about her. Tell me to keep quiet if I do the same with you."

"Keep quiet." She smiled.

"That's a pact then."

"Good."

To the driver, Lord Robert said, "Let's hear the weather forecast, please."

"Yes, milord," the driver said.

"Today's weather will be cloudy in the morning, giving way . . ."

There was a brief lull.

The same male voice said, "We interrupt the news to announce a special bulletin."

A pause ensued.

In a terse statement, the voice said, "The special branch of the Garda announces the mysterious disappearance of eighteen-year-old Fiona Morgan. She is described as a five-foot six-inch green-eyed blonde female weighing approximately eight and a half stone. She recently graduated from the Ursuline Boarding School, where her school friends remember her as a shy, brilliant student with an introspective nature. Her fondness for music was legendary. She disappeared from her guardian's house without a word. Foul play has not been ruled out. Anybody knowing her whereabouts, please call the Garda."

Fiona hoped that the inward panic she experienced could not be transmitted to Lord Robert. Outwardly she tried to remain calm. She put her index finger of her right hand to her lips, implying that she did not want the driver to know more than he needed. The weather forecast continued.

Lord Robert said, "Is that you they're after, Fiona?"

"It couldn't be."

"If it isn't you, who are they looking for?"

"I wish the driver would hurry," she whispered into his ear, and there was an imploring look in her eyes.

"He'll get you there, Fiona. Don't worry." He pressed her hand reassuringly, sending waves of excitement through her body.

"I'm worried. I've got to get out of Dublin promptly."

"May I ask if you were telling me the truth about yourself and the lord mayor?"

"Yes." There was annoyance in her voice.

"Are you Fiona, or is this an alias to hide dark secrets?"

"I am who I am. Believe me."

"Can I believe you?" he said, a smirk of his lips apparent. "Am I aiding and abetting a fugitive from justice?"

"If that's how you feel, I'll be glad to get out here in the midst of nowhere and go my way."

"Nonsense. You intrigue me even further. You're as mysterious as the night."

"Can I be more fascinating than you?"

"We all have our secrets to live with, torment us, to haunt us. I can attest to that. Perhaps I've said too much."

"You've said nothing that makes sense to me. Don't apologize."

"I wasn't about to ask your forgiveness, my dear." His voice was dripping with sarcasm.

"I'll be out of your life soon."

"Too bad." He said it as if he meant it. "Come closer to me. You need me as much as I need you."

Fiona was tormented by confusing emotions as Lord Robert nestled close to her. What was he implying by that statement? Was he trying to make her divulge more than she wished? Would he get out of the car and report her to the special Garda?

Lord Robert was bitter. His life seemed to be cloaked in secrecy. Was he trying to make Fiona buckle under his will? Was he a woman hater? She bristled at the whole concept of her present situation.

Fiona was almost totally oblivious to the towns, hamlets, villages, and farmyards that were but momentary glances as the car whizzed on and on. She realized that it was her turbulent frame of mind that was making her suspicious even of Lord Robert. Fiona thought of her father, and a sadness permeated her body, try as she might to banish it.

"Please forgive me, Robert," Fiona said, "but I'm thinking of my father."

"I know so little about you. Where is your father?"

"In America."

"That's a place that's always fascinated me. So young, so primitive, and yet so advanced. It attracts the best and the worst."

Then the light of angels seemed to surround her. Was this because she needed protection? Of course, she did. A cold sensation enveloped her, and all she could think of was her father. Times were so few when Fiona had met him, yet she couldn't wait each time to see him. What was she to do if anything happened to him? She must banish such grim thoughts. Was it because Fiona was overwrought that she worried about her father?

Considering Fiona's age, her father was not that young. In fact, he was in poor health and in his seventies. Never had Fiona doubted the depth of his love for her. She believed that there must be a reason why he could not see her as often as she would have liked. Then, of course, he was a man obsessed with work. It seemed to be his lifelong passion. He felt the company could not survive without him. For a man who had scraped himself up from poverty, he felt his company was a lifetime achievement. As he was wont to remind Fiona, times had not always been easy for him.

Lord Robert pressed Fiona's hand reassuringly. Such waves of rapture tingled through her fingers and palm that she wanted to remain intertwined with him. She had not felt anything so wondrous and glorious before. And the mounting sensations remained with her.

Fiona pulled her hand away abruptly. She must not succumb to desires that heretofore she had not known.

"How are you going to . . . manage in London?" he enquired.

"I haven't given it much thought yet," she stammered.

"It terrifies me to think how a young lady can survive without a job or other resources in such a fast-paced city."

"It frightens me even more."

"However," he sighed a long sigh, "you must sow your oats. It's an experience unto itself. Somehow I feel you'll do well."

"That's comforting that you should feel that way."

"Here's my address. I'd like to hear from you when you're settled in."

Fiona placed his address in a safe place in the middle pocket of her handbag. She realized that he was the only person to whom she could turn for help. Moreover, he was someone who meant more than others to her. Why? To that she did not have an answer, save to say she was extremely lucky to have survived the night in Bedford Castle.

Fiona recalled how pleasantly surprised she had been when Lord Robert said he would accompany her to Dublin. Was this how such a nobleman treated every woman?

CHAPTER 6

Now that Lord Von Pragh should be grieving about his wife when he had the world literally at his feet, Fiona wondered why women weren't flocking around him. By his own admission, they had attempted to be close to him, and he had discouraged it. Was it his fault, or could there be a mysterious force, the Lady Christiana Von Pragh standing between him and them?

Was it possible that Lady Christiana had been a very possessive person in life who could not part with Lord Von Pragh in death? The idea made her shudder. If this had happened to others, why should it not happen to Fiona? Of course, it was preposterous to entertain the notion. And yet what proof did Fiona have that it did not exist? Secretly she hoped that she too would leave such a lasting impression on a husband. Of course, this was out of the question now. Mundane matters were staring her in the face, such as where she would sleep tonight and thereafter in London.

It was pointless to try to banish these grim forebodings. Fiona must face stark reality. She was a wanted woman by the police. She had no one to turn to. Her grandmother had been very explicit in telling her to go to London. She feared serious retribution if this advice were not followed. And here she was, sitting beside the most handsome, aloof blind friend whom she was sure could use his influence to extricate her from this present predicament.

Fiona was certain that if she sent a telegram to her father for money, he would forward it immediately. The crux of the matter was that she had never known his address.

Throughout life, Fiona's surrogate mother had forwarded all correspondence to him. Fiona had not known his address, and still did not. Realizing that the United States of America was a big place, Fiona had no idea where in Virginia her father lived.

She plucked up courage and said, "Do you have any friends in London who could perhaps watch over me, Robert?"

"Yes. Yes. Too many of them. They live lives you haven't dreamed. These men are young, powerful, wealthy, some with titles. Young blokes are a dime a dozen in London."

"Hmm!"

"The chaps I know lead fast and furious lives, hop from one woman to another, go to too many parties, and leave many a girl with a broken heart. That lifestyle is all right when you're single. I was part of it, I'm sorry to say. Then love intervened."

"How old were you?"

"Twenty-seven. Old enough to know my mind, you might say."

"And your life changed when you met Christiana."

"Absolutely. From the moment we met, I knew I wanted her to be my wife. Strangely enough, even though I kept it to myself, she knew too I was the man for her. Somehow women sense this sort of phenomena."

"Oh! I believe that."

"Of course you do. On the first night we met, I told her she was the woman I would marry one day."

"Did she believe you?"

"She did. It was as if we communicated in body and soul from the beginning."

"I suspect you still commune with her in spirit."

"You're right. We do. And who knows, we may till we meet again."

A twinge of jealousy pricked at Fiona. Christiana was dead, she told herself. Did she still influence him?

"Enough about Christiana," he said.

"You promised not to talk about her," she said, her tone reproachful.

"So I did."

Again Lord Robert touched Fiona's hand, causing her breasts to heave tumultuously within her bodiced wine-colored silk dress. He moved closer and kissed her on the cheek. Then his mouth, hard and firm, sought Fiona's. She wanted to resist, but his mouth was on her lips, kissing her, commanding her silently.

Fiona's mind reeled in ecstasy at the tumult within her. This should not be, this shall not be, she reminded herself. And the wondrous heavenly sensations flooded through her body. As she became increasingly pliant and submissive, she felt Robert's hard, firm body pressing against her, touching the silk of her dress, probing her mouth till she was lost in the wonder and glory of his kisses.

For Fiona it was a moment of divine transformation to be lifted and soared to such realms of glory. Suddenly Fiona felt a cold sensation. A veiled creature or a ghostly being, definitely something not of this world, stood between them.

Lord Robert pulled away.

Fiona sat in shocked disbelief. Even though she realized her hair was in disarray, she stared at Lord Robert. He did not utter a word. He gazed into Fiona's eyes as she tried to avert them. Averting them was to no avail. She believed she detected a sparkle, yes, a sparkle that she had not seen before.

"Why . . . did you move . . . away?" she enquired.

There was a pause before he ensued. "I went . . . too . . . far."

"That was . . . the only . . . reason?" She was still joyous at the impact of his kiss.

"Why? Why do you . . . ask?" he asked, his face flushed and hair awry.

"I thought . . . maybe . . . I'm wrong . . . there was another reason."

"No. No."

"Are you sure?" There was earnestness in her voice.

"What are you trying to say?"

"I had the . . . strange feeling that something . . . somebody . . . I don't know what to call it, interrupted you."

"I don't believe what you're saying."

"I'm not . . . believe me, I'm not . . . losing my senses."

"I know I don't have that power over you. Do I?" There was an impish grin of his face.

"Seriously though, didn't you notice anything . . . strange . . . while we were kissing?"

"I was intoxicated with you." His smile was more infectious.

Fiona was thrilled to hear this but tried to conceal her delight. "I'm telling you, Robert, something came between us."

"Nonsense."

"It wasn't my imagination."

"How many times have you kissed to be able to tell the difference?"

"Only my father." There was a sob in her voice. "I fear you don't believe me."

"You're a child of fantasy."

"Am I?"

"Let's drop the subject. You're too sensitive, and you shouldn't let your imagination be carried away by one kiss. It's that spiritual quality of yours. Many men will kiss you in London. Please remember I'll miss you."

"I'll miss you too."

Was Lord Robert sincere? Fiona wondered. She knew she meant it from the bottom of her heart. As preposterous as the situation seemed, Fiona was convinced that what she had experienced had not been a mere coincidence.

CHAPTER 7

Lord Robert was hiding something. Why this reaction? Had this happened before? Was he afraid that Fiona would be frightened by it? Of course, Fiona was disturbed by it. What person in her right frame of mind would not have been? she reasoned.

The question is, Had Fiona been in an altered state of mind? Undoubtedly, the kiss she had experienced had lifted her to dizzying heights. Yet she had an uncanny sense that the veil, the mist, whatever she could call it, had been real—as real as if a person, a ghost, another worldly being, had stepped in, had blocked her path.

To whom could Fiona relate such a tale? As nonsensical as it may sound to someone else, it had seemed as authentic as someone switching a light off. But it had not been the mere physical presence she had experienced. It was the cold sensation accompanying it, as if ushering in a gust of wind, which enveloped her. While the whole concept seemed totally outlandish, Fiona was convinced that yes, something had intervened when she became responsive to Lord Robert's magical kiss.

Instantly Fiona tried to banish the matter from her mind. Any sane person listening to such a tale would say she was bonkers. She had enough trials without compounding them with this story, which any human being would regard as a fabrication.

Thinking of a human being was the crux of the matter in Fiona's mind. This intervention by whomever or whatever was definitely not a human being. This ghost was not of this world. Had it ever been? Of this Fiona was sure. The ghost was a woman, a very beautiful, statuesque woman, a woman who had lived on this earth before. She seemed tranquil in the way she glided between Fiona and Robert.

Although jealous, Fiona felt she must not harbor ill will towards this ghost. There must have been a reason that the ghost appeared at such an inopportune moment. Was the ghost trying to convey an important message? Was she trying to warn her? Perhaps she was trying to give an inkling about an unsavory aspect of Robert's nature. After all, Fiona hardly knew Lord Robert. Was there a big dark secret looming over his head?

Had Lord Robert wronged a woman in the past in love? Had this ghost been jilted in her lifetime by Lord Robert? Fiona knew that beings of the spirit world had been known to roam this earth. For what? Why was this spirit not at rest like others who had passed over? Had Lord Robert been the cause of this spirit's murder or some foul deed? Who knows? Fiona was not about to find out now.

CHAPTER 8

In the distance, Fiona heard the swish of honking cars over the wet streets. The driver drove through the evening rush hour with traffic crawling at a snail's pace in the city of Dublin. Oblivious to the streetlights, office workers appeared to be in no hurry to get home. Others sauntered into smoke-filled pubs. Bells tolled from a nearby church. The pungent smell of the river Liffey assaulted Fiona's nostrils.

"Where would you like me to go, milord?" the driver enquired.

"Directly to Dun Laoghaire," Lord Van Pragh said. "We'll find out when the boat leaves."

On and on they went to the outskirts of Dublin. Fiona was at a loss for words. She knew she wanted to get to know Lord Van Pragh better. Obviously it was not meant to be. More so, she believed, because of the spirit entity. So much inner turmoil made the trip seem very fast.

The driver was now driving through the pier gates, which were flung open. He parked the car convenient to the ticket office. He rushed back.

"The boat leaves in half an hour," he said. "I have the ticket for the lady."

When Lord Van Pragh and Fiona got out of the car, she attempted to straighten out her clothes, which had been literally ripped off her back. Both walked a short distance towards the gangplank, the fierce winds almost carrying them along. She wasn't sure whether a policeman lurking in a doorway was admiring her or wondering whether she was the woman in question that the special branch of the Garda had put out an all search bulletin. The thought frightened her.

Fiona was afraid to confide the information to Lord Von Pragh. She was quite sure that the cacophony of sounds in the shrill wind made it virtually impossible for her to confide in him. Her long blonde hair whipped against her cheeks and across her eyes.

At the entrance to the gangplank, Lord Von Pragh said, fishing in his trouser pocket, "Take this, Fiona. It's very old and means nothing to me anymore."

"Oh! I cannot."

He brushed her protest aside. "I want you to have this. Wear it. You'll need luck in London."

"Thank you very much."

Fiona glanced at the very old green stone no bigger than the tip of the ring finger of her hand.

"My great-great-grandfather found this on an archeological dig in Egypt. The Egyptians believed this stone had healing power. One thing it never did was restore my sight."

"You can do that," Fiona said, looking him directly in the eyes.

"I want you to remember me when you look at this wherever you are."

"Your kindness is truly appreciated."

There was commotion with people hurrying to get to the ship.

"You must make haste, Fiona," Lord Von Pragh said.

He kissed her cold cheek briefly but tenderly. She felt fire stirring within this man. Despite his cold, aloof demeanor, he seemed to be protecting Fiona and ensuring that her plans did not get muddled. It was precisely the type of person she needed—a decisive man who didn't hem and haw about matters. Outwardly brimming with confidence, it was a far cry from how Fiona felt.

Under the patient glow of the gas light, Fiona would have been thrilled to get to know Lord Von Pragh better. She thought maybe it was destiny. Perhaps she could never replace a woman who loved him so dearly that even after such a long lapse of time, Lord Von Pragh pined for her. How Fiona wished she could have such a powerful influence on him.

Her luggage aboard, Fiona watched the cold near-dusk mist envelop Lord Von Pragh as the boat pulled out of Dun Laoghaire harbor to the choppy waters of the Atlantic Ocean. How easily she could identify with him alone.

Fiona was tossed back on the deck when she stepped on a man's foot.

"Wow!" he shouted.

"I'm very sorry," she said.

He smiled as he prevented her from falling.

"Do that again," he said.

Fiona retreated to the main lounge where a group of men sat discussing art. She heard one man talking about the up and coming artist in Amsterdam who had taken the art world by storm with the introduction of a painting of a field of flowers. They discussed that while the man was extremely gifted, he was too emotional for his own good.

Among the group was a young dark-haired bearded man who ogled every female in the lounge. Fiona was not flattered by the brazen way he stared at her. She was tempted to stare back but decided to keep a low profile. Later on she learned from the captain, who showed a special interest in her, that he was the foremost painter from Spain.

Up to now, Fiona had been under the assumption that she was well versed in many subjects. She realized that she was quite ignorant about art. Part of that stemmed from the fact that her father had wanted her reared and educated in a provincial town to protect her. That, he had admittedly done. She had learned about horses and saw her father's own being trained by the trainer who raced horses in the Grand National and Kentucky Derby on flat green land that stretched for miles. Yet Tipperary had given her no exposure to art. In fact, Fiona had never been to an art gallery. How insecure she would feel in London with the sophisticated, if not somewhat depraved, men Lord Von Pragh had described to her.

It seemed little time had lapsed before the announcer over the intercom said, "Passengers going to Southampton will change boats at Holyhead."

Fiona boarded the other ship. The lowly mournful cries of a foghorn rent the stillness of the night. Settled in the lounge, Fiona thought of Robert. How she wished he were accompanying her to London. She realized all too clearly that she was alone, without anyone to turn to.

A babble of languages was spoken on the ship from Welsh to Indian to Turkish. This was a new life, but nevertheless, she thought it could be fraught with danger.

Suddenly Fiona recalled her grandmother's apparition. Maybe it was a wise move that she was making to London. So many dark secrets seemed to lurk in Lord Von Pragh's background. Yet it could be that he didn't know Fiona well enough to confide in her. She was determined to change his mind.

CHAPTER 9

At Southampton, Fiona disembarked quickly. Seagulls circled the ship in the hope of a handout. People were congregated at dockside, waiting for loved ones. As she was in the queue for the train, a fortyish grey-headed bespectacled man approached her.

"Heading to the big city, are you?" he said in a Welsh accent.

"Yes. I'm going to London."

"Are you from London?"

"No. It's my first trip."

"You must be excited."

"I'm a bit nervous."

"That's only natural."

"It's my first time away from home."

"Could you do me a very big favor?"

"That depends." She smiled wryly.

"I'm weighed down with luggage. I've a document that must arrive in London this evening or at the very least tomorrow morning."

"Can't you wire it?"

"It would take me out of my way very much. I'm extremely busy."

Fiona gasped at the outrageous sum of money the man was willing to give her. Inwardly she thought the contents must be of the utmost urgency. Besides, she should certainly be able to find accommodation with that money.

"I'll take it," she said, her heart leaping with pleasure.

From a locked suitcase, he retrieved a rolled package, which was well wrapped with black paper.

"I'll make arrangements," he said, "for Mr. Justine Smith to meet you at Paddington market. Mr. Smith is an older hunchbacked man who is five feet tall. You can't miss him. He always wears a cap pulled down over his ear. He sustained some kind of ear injury in World War I, which left himself conscious about having only one ear. Strangely enough, he is recognized by the red cap. Everyone knows him."

"Sounds as if he's quite a character."

"That he is. I never really knew his exact age. That man knows London like the back of his hand. He's a true Cockney born within the sound of Bow Bells."

"I hear the true Cockney is very difficult to understand."

"Never mind that. Take care of my package. See that Justine gets it and no one else."

"Definitely."

"Have a wonderful trip. I hear the train coming."

It seemed no length of time till Fiona was in the heart of the city of London. For some inexplicable reason, she felt lighthearted and gay. If only Lord Von Pragh were beside her. Outside Paddington station with her package as she walked along the narrow cobbled streets, Fiona hardly imagined that so many people could be congregated in one place. So many different languages were spoken as she passed people scurrying hither and yon.

The town crier shouted, "Mother bludgeoned in Holloway prison for starving her child to death!"

Fiona experienced a cold sensation and passed on quickly to drown out the details. The lamp lighter was atop a pole lighting the gas lamps. She felt a sensation of being totally at home in such a gay city. This was obviously a place where a person's aspirations, no matter how lofty, were not frowned upon. And Fiona's aspirations were to become an opera singer. As a child, she was often told that she had a voice that could make angels weep.

The brisk wind blowing the treetops put renewed vigor into her step. When she arrived at Covent Garden, she stood in awe of the building of Elizabethan architecture whose walls had wrought every emotion in millions of opera lovers over the years. Oblivious to the flower sellers and drunks and prostitutes who predominated the neighborhood, she observed the heavy doors and visualized herself walking through them one day. No doubt it would be a long time before this. Her mind wasn't totally in the clouds.

It was the roar of the crowd within those sacrosanct walls that Fiona yearned. Although insecure deep within, her voice could transcend the loneliness and despair that she had often felt in childhood. Convinced that this must be a tough city to survive, she vowed to attain her goals.

Several extremely handsome men glanced at Fiona with a look of curiosity, if not admiration. And why not? she thought. She must appear like a *hick* from the country, which was a polite term for someone who grew up surrounded by farmland and horses. But that was behind Fiona now, as she moved on and tread gingerly through the streets. She glanced at the shops with sophisticatedly dressed mannequins.

In a warehouse section, Fiona passed a pack of mangy-looking and somewhat bloodied dogs and was moved by their plight. She wished she had a few steak bones she could throw them. Further along was Covent Garden marketplace, with blood from the fish running in the street.

There were cockles and mussels and goat cheese, tins of biscuits, pans of every description, earthenware hot-water bottles, fire bellows, cheap perfume, and virtually anything that was saleable.

The red-caped man was not difficult to spot. The brilliant red cap he was wearing stood out like a beacon among the crowd. Fiona walked up to him past a customer haggling over the price of a cuckoo clock that looked like it was ready to fall to pieces.

"Good evening!" Fiona said. "You have to be Mr. Justine Smith."

"Yep," he said in a low, gravelly, menacing tone of voice.

"This is the package." She handed it to him.

He put it in the crook of his arm and said, "What's your name?"

"Fiona Morgan."

"One of those damned and beautiful Irish women?"

Without further ado, Fiona headed to another street where a man speaking through a microphone shouted, "Praised be Jesus. Return to Jehovah. The end is near. The end is near. It's right at our doorstep. I was blind, but now I can see."

Fiona immediately thought of Lord Von Pragh and somehow visualized a miracle happening in his life. He could discard his cane and do anything he liked.

How wonderful it would be if he could see the triumph of the spirit of the people of London. That would take him out of his depression. In Tipperary he had so little to think about that he was obsessed with a dead wife. If he could only see the tall buildings being erected everywhere, which had been bombed during World War II.

The sense of nationalism and pride was enough to swell a man's heart and be proud to be British. Fiona's heart skipped a beat as a black maria halted parallel to her. Police with night sticks jumped out. A group of men dispersed in all directions, leaving a cardboard box and cards on the table. The police followed in whichever direction they had taken. The long-legged pursued males rushed into oncoming traffic, causing the irate taxi driver to honk the horn and zigzag to avoid hitting one and almost hitting the other, who kicked the taxi in retaliation.

Farther along at the corner of the square, a tall, thin angular man wearing a turban cried, "Out with the Conservatives. They go with the will of the people who want to ban immigration of Indians. They claim we take away their jobs. I say we do the dirty work the English feel is beneath their dignity."

A twentyish ragamuffin said, "Shut up, you blighter. No more Indians. We want work. Charity begins at home."

"Aye! Aye!" a chorus of voices rose in unison.

A fistfight ensued amongst liberals and laborers. Others fled the scene, and Fiona found herself running with the pack. She thought she had better be careful and hold on to her handbag, lest her newfound wealth disappeared with all the pushing and shoving.

Fiona wound around street after street with lights on in some houses while others were still in darkness. A man in his sixties with grey hair, blue eyes, and jolly cheeks stopped Fiona in her tracks.

"Are you lost, young lady?" he enquired.

"In a way. I'm new to London."

"I thought so. The evenings get dark early now. You have to be careful roaming these streets alone. Where do you want to go?"

Fiona hemmed and hawed for a few minutes. She said, "I'm looking for a place to stay."

"A beautiful young lady like you should have no trouble."

"It's a question of finances. Do you know of a reasonable place? I don't want to spend all my money for a boarding house."

"Naturally."

"It's not that I'm impoverished. I'm not. But I don't have a job yet. I've to eat and live."

"Don't be ashamed to say if you don't have money. In itself money means little if you're not happy."

"That's true."

"You look like a well-bred person. If I may be impertinent to say that you're welcome to stay in my house."

"I've some money. I can pay you now."

"Nonsense. If I need it, I'll ask you."

"I'd like to repay you in some way."

"Money should be the least worry. I've a nice house. It's too big and sometimes lonely without the children and grandchildren around."

"My name is Fiona Morgan."

"Delighted to meet you, Fiona. I'm Charles Phelps."

There was something about the man's mannerisms and frankness that put Fiona distinctly at ease. They chatted away as if they had known each other at another time, rather than as strangers. Fiona did not rule out the possibility that they could have met in a previous life, such as reincarnation.

A man with a limp and a cane saluted Fiona's newfound companion. Fiona and Charles walked about five blocks to their destination in Penrose Mews in Kensington. White lace curtains were blowing in many windows. Dogs barked from some houses and flats. Independent cats sat peacefully in windows. The area was near to the hustle and bustle yet removed enough that one could not be disturbed by honking cars and subjected to the fumes of the double-decker buses.

Charles fumbled in his pocket and unlocked the front door. A spry terrier wagged his tail and greeted Charles first and sniffed Fiona. Satisfied that Fiona was not an intruder, the terrier leapt back into a rumpled, cozy chair. Charles stoked some life into the fire.

From somewhere, a voice said, "Hello."

Fiona turned around, puzzled by the voice. She was not prone to auditory hallucinations, or was it due to the fact that she was in a different city divorced from the true and familiar?

Again Fiona heard "Hello."

She looked around, baffled by the unknown. Sitting on a perch in a cage was a brilliant-green-and-yellow macaw.

Charles straightened up from blowing the bellows and said, "Is Greta bothering you?"

"Oh no. I was surprised to hear a voice from apparently nowhere."

"Everybody is at first upset and then fascinated by Greta. She's a wonderful bird."

The macaw chirped merrily and said, "Lovely bird, Charlie. Lovely bird." She cooed and preened like a seductive temptress.

"Don't prattle on, Greta. This is . . . let me see if I remember your name."

Fiona felt she would have to refresh Charles's memory. "Fiona is the name."

"Yes. Yes. That's it. My brain is getting foggy with age."

"Mine will one day." She winked mischievously.

"You're a long way from that."

"Age catches up with all of us."

"Have as much fun as you can, Fiona. You're only young once."

An assortment of hardbound books lined the shelves. A large number of them were about birds and bird watching. Charles reminded her that she could cook anything in the kitchen as long as she washed the dishes.

Leading the way, Charles said, "This is my son's room." There was a gleam of pride in his eyes.

Boyhood photographs were scattered on the walls. A hockey stick splintered with age and a ball rested in the corner. There were pictures of his mother and father on the dressing table in heart-shaped frames.

"Make yourself at home, Fiona," Charles said. "This is your room."

"It's absolutely lovely and so spacious."

There were two large bay windows opposite each other. One faced the garden, and the other faced the street.

"Why don't you lie down?" Charles said. You must be weary after such a trip."

"A little. I'll take your advice."

"Do that."

Fiona lay down on the bed, and her thoughts went out to Lord Von Pragh. Gone were the days when he could play hockey with friends. Gone were the days when he could walk the lanes and byways without considering stumbling. Gone were the days when he could sit at home with his cherished wife. Gone were the days when he could make love to her. Everything he had struggled for had seemed inconsequential. He must have thought life would go merrily onward till a ripe old age weakened their limbs and they would have each other to lean on.

Fiona thought it must be very lonely for him, as she tried to visualize what he was doing across the Atlantic Ocean. Her heart reached out to him. She must drop him a note as soon as she awakened, telling him that she had arrived safely. That had been his request, and she must abide by it.

It would, of course, be wonderful to have Robert in bed lying beside her, to glow in the warmth of his touch, to not be puzzled by the spirit entity of his beloved wife. Each time she remembered it, she was jealous, inordinately jealous, considering he had entered her life a short time ago.

Would Fiona's love for Robert grow further if she saw him again? Perhaps new surroundings would snap him out of his depression. A top Harley street specialist should be able to restore his sight. Why not even resort to unconventional methods to restore his sight?

Any method was better than no method. Fiona had read about natural healing. While she was in London she would learn about it and possibly practice it. She was aware that natural healers meditated on a daily basis. Perhaps with love and undying affection, she could make Robert see. Of course, she doubted that it was possible, and yet there remained a facet that said it was indeed possible.

By now she assumed that Rory McCormack must be seething with rage on the realization that Fiona had skedaddled to avoid marriage. If Fiona were to entertain the idea of marriage, it would be to no one but Lord Robert Von Pragh. He had been her rescuer in time of trial. God knows he had his own tribulations to contend with besides being burdened with Fiona's. Maybe it was for this reason he had helped her. His heart seemed to reach out to her in its somewhat gruff way.

Fiona could not help but make excuses for Robert. Admittedly, she had interfered with his silent communication with Christiana. More than likely she had been the first and only person allowed to enter the chapel. That in itself was a step forward for her. And she thought if his wife had loved him so passionately, shouldn't she be able to part with him and allow him to go on living a normal life? Couldn't her love for him help to restore his sight from the grave? More than likely she was his spirit guide protecting him.

Was it possible that Lord Von Pragh's deceased wife wanted to protect him from being hurt by another woman? If that was her motive, surely it was admirable. Fiona must gather her wits and not think strictly of herself. But she reminded herself that she wanted Lord Robert to be gay, worldly, and living like a normal man. Cooped up in the country with memories seemed to enmesh him in a depression, which, if not handled, could be more serious.

Certain that she had Lord Robert's best interests at heart, Fiona must make him realize that life must go on. He must live a joyous life. With these thoughts, she drifted into a deep slumber. Wasn't Lord Robert entitled to the best?

CHAPTER 10

Charles was reading the *London Times* while the dog, Dubois, rested on his slipper and Greta chirped merrily from a windowsill. Fiona was sitting at the kitchen table, when suddenly there was a knock at the door. Dubois leapt to the door. Who could it be, she wondered, at such an early hour? She had nothing to fear. She opened the door. Standing on the doorstep was Lord Robert Von Pragh.

Fiona's luminous eyes widened in astonishment. Although she tried to stifle it, a soft gasp escaped her. Appearing more animated than before, Lord Von Pragh's eyes seemed to be searching her very essence.

"I was so worried about you alone in London that I decided to see you were settled in," he said.

"How very considerate of you."

"Not at all. I always enjoyed London, although I've lost some of my friends. Marriage changed that."

"Won't you come in," she said, embarrassed about how awful she must look so early.

Without knowing why, Fiona felt his eyes watch her every movement. She excused herself, thinking she should comb her hair. Realizing it was ill mannered to keep him waiting in the hallway unnecessarily, she hurried to the master of the house.

"Charles, may I bring in a friend?" she said.

"The more young people in the house, the merrier. Please come in."

Fiona introduced Lord Von Pragh and Charles.

"Robert, would you like a cup of tea while I'm making breakfast for you?" Fiona enquired.

"Only if I can come to the kitchen to be near you."

His appeal awakened a passionate message within Fiona. The nearness of his body unnerved her. Why must she succumb to the charms of a man who was an enigma? Then that cold feeling, that spirit, seemed to flash before Fiona's eyes. Was this spirit getting out of control and trying to confront Fiona?

Since she had left him in Ireland, Fiona had not felt that presence. It was a transatlantic spirit. It was associated with Robert, and only him. Wasn't it sufficient that she had one person to contend with rather than two?

Somehow she suspected that Lord Von Pragh was as fully aware of the spirit as Fiona.

When she no longer felt the presence, she said, "You're the last person I expected to see here, Robert."

"I've nothing to hold me down anymore. I'm a free man."

"Are you truly free, Robert?"

"When is one free? No longer do I have attachments. My wife has been dead for two years. I'll have to get over it. I suppose there's nothing better than a change of scenery. Believe me, visiting a vault every night is not considered normal. I'm no psychologist or psychiatrist. Common sense tells me that. I'm probably not the most sensible person in the world."

"That's not the impression I have of you."

"No doubt you think I'm a sentimental old fool. Be that as it may, I've decided to put the past behind me and be near to you in London. We'd make a good couple."

Fiona gasped in astonishment at Lord Von Pragh's frankness. Had he taken leave of his senses? She was utterly thrilled and astounded to hear this coming from his lips, those lips—soft, sensual, and vulnerable. Fiona's heart almost skipped a beat.

Something was happening to Fiona that had not happened before. Was she falling in love? Why did Lord Von Pragh arouse in her such depths of desire that heretofore had been alien to her? She felt ill equipped to deal with love. Her mind in a quandary, she was hardly able to concentrate on the cooking.

Yet Fiona's desire to please Lord Von Pragh was uppermost in her mind. She wanted to be the perfect woman to meet his requirements. And yet she thought he was probably an exacting man.

Fiona excused herself while she went to the garden. There she cut off some hyacinth flowers. Inside she arranged them in a vase and placed them on the dining room table. Even though Lord Von Pragh couldn't see, she was sure he would appreciate the fragrant-smelling flowers. Intoxicated with him, she led the way into the dining room, with him leaning on her arm.

Despite the fact that the food was delicious and served on the best sparkling china, Fiona was only capable of eating a small portion. She listened to everything Lord Von Pragh had to say, and it was music to her ears.

"After you left," Lord Von Pragh said, 'I knew I wasn't going to meet a special person like you again. Am I special to you?"

She was ready to blurt out yes but decided to hold back. This was a sophisticated, worldly man. He knew the right things to say at the right time. He knew how to please a woman, how to put her on a pedestal. Was that what he was doing to Fiona? She could fall head over heels in love with Lord Von Pragh. Life couldn't be that simple. It would take its twists and turns, some of them thorny and a few smooth.

And yet Fiona was convinced that this was not a gentleman who loved easily. There must have been beautiful women in his life within the last two years. Why had they left? Had they experienced Christiana's spirit when they touched Lord Von Pragh? Like Fiona, were they afraid of getting to know him better?

This was the point. Fiona was at the mercy of his wife. It was impossible to tell Lord Von Pragh that he meant more to her than she cared to divulge. How she wished she could bare her heart and soul to him. Would it change circumstances? Maybe in the past he had at great length spoken about his wife till a woman friend concluded that it was hopeless situation.

Yet Fiona thought it must be heaven for such a man to love so deeply. His feelings must be so intense like a simmering volcano once stroked could not stop but erupt into an abiding love. Fiona seriously wondered as she watched Lord Von Pragh eat his breakfast with relish that he could love her.

When Robert had finished his tea, he said, "Fiona, you don't know what it's like dying in the country."

"Yes. You were. Dying of grief is almost like physical death. It drains us of our energy."

"You're too young to know this."

"I'm eighteen."

"I'm twenty-eight."

"Twenty-eight isn't that old."

"For the last couple of years, I've felt like one hundred years of age. When I saw you young and adventuresome setting forth, I thought this is a young lady I want to know better."

"You're very flattering."

"I mean it." His voice was grave. "What can I offer you? Absolutely nothing."

"You have yourself."

"I feel you radiate a spirituality that one associates with saints."

"Hush! You don't mean that."

"I do. I feel it anytime you're near me. The crassness of life seems to have eluded you."

Embarrassed, Fiona hurried upstairs, bathed quickly, and took great pains within a very short period of time to make sure she was looking wonderful. Because she was well rested, her skin was glowing with a porcelain radiance. Her hair pulled back in a black bow, soft tendrils framed her face accentuating the emerald hue of her eyes. She wore a mother-of-pearl choker around her neck, which Charles loaned to her. The fitted bodice of the dress accentuated the whiteness of her bosom.

When Fiona arrived in the dining room, Robert waited for her as if by rote. She assumed he must have heard the rustle of her dress descending the staircase.

"Let's take a walk in the garden," he suggested.

The odor of cedar from his jacket seemed to emanate in the wind as Robert took her hand as they walked down three stone steps. With his cane, she led the way past squirrels, who sat upright on the bench, begging for food. There was a male and female. They scurried up an oak tree and appeared to be enjoying themselves. Fiona felt the coolness of Robert's left hand.

"Are you cold?" she enquired.

"No. I'm a red-hot-blooded male." He winked mischievously.

They moved to a nearby boat. With assistance, Robert stepped in. Swans glided gracefully while he sat near her.

"Did you know, Fiona, that swans mate for life? If one dies, the other does not mate again."

"Interesting!" she commented. "It must be very lonely treading the waters on its own."

"That's loyalty, my dear."

Was Robert trying to drop a hint? How many times and in how many ways did she have to be reminded? He was a total enigma. Were they his words, or was he silently communing with Christiana? She was afraid to ask, lest he become irritated and more than likely deny it.

Fiona held his left hand. Gradually she felt warmth exuding from it. Such quivers of excitement tingled up and down her spine that Fiona felt she must control herself. Far too sophisticated for her liking, she must dampen her enthusiasm for him. He dropped his cane and put her hand on his muscular thigh. She felt the tautness of his body. Gently he lifted her head and kissed her tenderly on the lips. His mouth probed hers. It seemed an eternity before he released her. Such wondrous, glorious feelings flooded through her body that she tried to suppress. But it was to no avail. She moved closer to him.

Robert grabbed her more desperately, moving his hand down to his swollen penis. It seemed to be pulsing with desire. Fiona felt her body weaken, and stirrings within her such as she had never felt before. Were these the embodiment of a troubled young woman or a love that could transcend time?

In his mind's eye was Robert comparing Fiona to Christiana? More than likely he was. The mere musical sound of her name aroused in Fiona a jealously of such magnitude that it could overwhelm her. No. She must be staunch. She must not let this first inexperienced love get out of proportion. She was a woman. He was a man with inner urgings accentuated by the fact that he had been grieving and blind for two years.

Fiona's body and mind yearned for Robert. Was it possible that she could arouse in him the depths of desire that he had shared with Christiana? Nonsense, she presumed. She was just a lonely person seeking love where she had never been before. Oh! How heavenly it was.

Yes. Fiona was not realistic. She had been reminded only a few minutes ago that Robert was destined to stay alone. He was in a predicament beset by blindness. She was escaping a man bent on marrying her—the repulsive Rory McCormack.

Fiona felt the warmth of his genitals as he caressed her hand closer.

"I bet you're a superb lover once you let your guard down," he whispered. "We could make the heavens thunder."

Fiona shuddered. There was no obvious change in the weather. She felt the spurt and thrust of Robert. Her hand was moist from his pants. He leaned back and let out a sigh. She kissed him ever so gently.

Again that cold waft of air slapped Fiona in the face with such force that she knew could only be the hand of Christiana. *Damn it!* she thought. Yes. Christiana was a force to be reckoned with. It was Robert who smiled with a look of satisfaction.

Had Fiona defied the charms of Christiana's influence over Robert?

Her musings were interrupted, when out of nowhere Robert said, "I shall remember and savor this when I'm in Ischia. Not the healing waters and the nubile young things whose parents introduce to me will make me forget this memory."

"I'm not likely to forget either," she murmured. "When oh when are you going to the Mediterranean coast?" There was a pleading tone to her voice.

"This evening at six o'clock. My aunt Lady Isabella hasn't seen me since I was in the Royal Air Force."

There and then Fiona's hopes were dashed. Who was she to think that she could sever the bond between Christiana and Robert? No. Fiona must not despair. She had moments of unbounded joy with Robert. She must be grateful for small mercies. Hadn't it been drilled into her head at the Ursuline boarding school that this life was meant for suffering? Yet her suffering was miniscule compared to that of Robert's. He must see once more the wonders and glories of the world.

Robert picked up his cane, stinging himself on a nettle. The sky darkened. Trees shivered violently. Suddenly large raindrops started to splatter on the stone pavement. Within a few minutes, a torrential rain released its fury, forcing them to make a hasty retreat to the house. The white and black swans maintained their course, gliding slowly by, unfettered by nature's turbulence.

Like a bolt of lightning, Fiona's grandmother's apparition flashed before her eyes. Reminding herself that London was a lucky location for her gave her renewed confidence. Would her grandmother's words prove to be true or false?

CHAPTER 11

It seemed no length of time before the driver appeared to pick up Lord Von Pragh. The sun shone fitfully as Fiona stood in the sitting room.

"I'll be back in a fortnight," Lord Von Pragh said. "Then we'll have some time together."

"I'm going to miss you very much, Robert," Fiona said.

"No, you won't. You'll be too busy looking for a job and dating cads who will promise you everything."

Robert kissed Fiona briefly. Such wondrous, rapturous feelings emanated through her body that it ached. Then he was gone as she watched the car glide down the street, heading to Heathrow Airport. A fortnight seemed an eternity before she would see him again.

That night as she was outstretched on her bed, Fiona's mind was in a quandary. Uppermost in her thoughts was the possibility of never seeing Lord Von Pragh. He could meet another woman. It pained her to think about it. Maybe he had a date with some beautiful, sophisticated world traveler. She had read in novels about men who lived that type of life.

Yet Lord Von Pragh had gone to extremes to find Fiona. Didn't that mean something significant? Of course, it did. Certain that he would not be interested like Fiona, who must seem a burden, she resolved to find employment. She wanted to make her mark in the world and be independent. But she did not have the wherewithal to accomplish that task. If she wrote to her father, he would wire her some money. He always had her best interest at heart. What if Lord Von Pragh drowned in the ocean at Ischia?

Then Fiona would have no one. She said a silent prayer to her grandmother. So many questions preoccupied her mind. What if she never saw him again? There was always that possibility. However, she must banish such morbid thoughts. Too many ifs, ands, and buts were revolving in her head. Why oh why must love be so complicated?

That was another question that she left to her imagination. Was Fiona so naïve to think that Lord Von Pragh would fall in love with her? What if Lord Von Pragh were kidnapped at the airport? How could he communicate with Fiona? What if he were mugged and robbed by thugs? He had no way of identifying them. A blind man traveling alone with a cane and luggage was preposterous and precarious, not to mention hopping into a taxi with an unknown driver who spoke no English. He could be dropped off and wind up in the midst of nowhere. The dangers were endless. What if he were attacked by a pack of hungry dogs and his aristocratic good looks destroyed?

Fiona was certain she would love Lord Von Pragh anyway. She must think kindly of humanity; otherwise, she would be a nervous wreck. Presumably, Lady Isabella had taken care of such possibilities. On the other hand, Lord Von Pragh had said she was getting old and not quite as competent as she used to be. Maybe he had devised a way of surviving since his blindness beset him.

Yet Lord Von Pragh seemed vulnerable to Fiona's way of thinking. What if he wound up in another part of the world? There they had seers and healers who were capable of restoring his vision. They used potions and concoctions foreign to the United Kingdom. In her darkest hour and with grim foreboding, Fiona meditated. Erelong she was drifting off to sleep.

Next day, Fiona could only think of Lord Von Pragh. Had he arrived safely in Ischia, where the weather was balmy? She knew that the island was surrounded by healing waters, healers, and mud baths and that the rich and pampered visited there. She managed to keep herself preoccupied by looking for a position. Then of course she was not trained for anything in particular. She would like to work around opera singing and music. It was in her blood; she had been repeatedly told by the Ursuline nuns.

As Fiona was glancing through the *Daily Mail*, she read, "Will Fiona Morgan, formerly of Tipperary, Ireland, kindly contact Thomas Dwyer, Esq. 22 High Street as soon as possible," followed by a phone number.

Fiona's heart skipped a beat. What could a lawyer want? Was this a ruse to find her and bring her back to Ireland and force her to marry the repulsive Rory McCormack? If it was, she would escape again. Whom could she get to answer the advertisement without revealing her whereabouts? She must tread cautiously.

Maybe Fiona's father had sought legal counsel when she did not answer his letter, assuming that he did write a letter. It seemed too much like coincidence that he should write when she had so recently left Ireland. Then, of course, he was not prone to writing that often. But she knew that her father loved her and certainly had her best interest at heart.

Could it be that the lady with whom she had lived for years was worried about her? Fiona was adamant that Rory McCormack had contacted her. It couldn't be Fiona's old school chums looking for her. Whoever it was seemed determined to find her when they had enlisted the aid of a lawyer. Who knows if the lawyer was honest? There had been rumors from time to time of unethical lawyers who resorted to underhanded measures on behalf of their clients. Fiona had no such dealings with such members of the law. However, she realized that boarding school and other financial matters were handled by one attorney in a large international law firm in Virginia.

There was no escape. Sooner or later, Fiona's whereabouts would be no secret. She had to apply for a position. She couldn't use an alias or other devious method. The police had ways of tracking down wanted persons. She was confident that the lawyer was not beyond doing the same to find her.

Fiona hoped Mr. Phelps hadn't seen the advertisement. He might think she was a wanted woman. For a moment she thought of the man who had paid her to deliver the small package in London. So many ideas were twirling around in Fiona's head that she didn't know where to begin. At the same time, she was worried for some unfathomable reason.

Why did the lawyer have to seek Fiona at this time and possibly jeopardize her relationship with Lord Von Pragh? She wondered if he had yet arrived in Ischia. There she would love to walk along the streets with him. She needed him now more than ever to confront this pesky situation with Thomas Dwyer, Esq. He would be able to handle the legal aspect more efficiently.

Charles Phelps would be Fiona's confidant. He would ensure nothing bad happened to her. She felt guilty that she hadn't paid him for his lodging, but she promised that as soon as she was gainfully employed, she would. When and where were matters over which she had little control now.

Fiona would trust her instincts and allow Mr. Phelps to contact the lawyer. When he came downstairs, she made him a pot of tea.

"Please read this, Charles," she pleaded.

"Hm!" he muttered between sips of tea with milk.

"Without telling him where I am, please find out what the lawyer wants."

"I'm sure if it's of a personal nature, he's not likely to tell me."

"In that case, I'll have to tell you the story up to this point. You see, Lord Von Pragh let me use his castle at a very inconvenient time. I ran away rather than marry Rory McCormack, the lord mayor of Limerick."

"I knew you'd never be alone, and that there were men who'd literally give their eye tooth for you."

"So you see the predicament."

"Yes. Let me see what I can do."

When Fiona returned from a walk in Hyde Park, Charles was sorry to inform her that no details could be furnished on the phone except to her.

Fiona called the law office of Dwyer and Dwyer.

Thomas Dwyer said, "Good morning, Ms. Morgan."

"Hello," Fiona said.

"I've been retained by your father's lawyer. I'm very sorry to inform you that your father has died."

Fiona felt the blood drain from her cheeks. She thought she was going to faint even though she was in a sitting position.

"He's already been buried, I believe, in Richmond," the barrister continued. "You must come to my office immediately. We have important matters to discuss."

"Couldn't it be done by post?"

"I'm afraid not. It is urgent that you be in my office two days from now. You'll have to allow yourself several hours to discuss your complicated father's will."

"I'm afraid I've very little money to travel."

"I'll personally deposit a bank check for two hundred pounds, which can be cashed immediately."

When Fiona got off the phone, she went to her room. Uncontrollable tears streamed down her cheeks. Her father had loved her so dearly, and she had worshipped him. To think that only now, she was informed of his death. If Fiona had been in Ireland, she wouldn't have missed his funeral in Richmond. Surely he had made arrangements for her to pay her respect. She blamed herself for the unforgiving act of nonattendance at his grave site.

Fiona's father was a true friend and father. She wept because of the few times she'd seen him. She wished she could have helped him on the many occasions when he gasped for breath. How right her instinctive feeling was that she'd never see him alive again. Why did God have to take such a wonderful human being? He was seventy-three years old, but that wasn't that old.

Even if Fiona's father had been one hundred years of age, he would always be the loving, trusted person she had met on too few occasions. Now he was gone. Never again would she hear the loving reassurances that she had meant more than life to him. This she knew to be true.

Wiping her eyes, Fiona felt utterly lost. How she wished she could have contacted her father prior to his death. Or was it a blessing that he didn't have to gasp for air each time he walked particularly in the hot weather.

Without thinking any further, Fiona went to St. Paul's Cathedral and had a Mass said for him. She also lit a candle and prayed that his soul had gone to heaven. Then she sat for half an hour and prayed and wept for the one person who truly loved her.

Fiona recalled the hectic schedule her father maintained and how he had tried to hide it when he was with her. He had wanted their time together to be precious, to be remembered. It was with such fondness and a sense of tranquility that Fiona walked out of St. Paul's Cathedral. Fiona also thought of Lord Von Pragh and how devastating his life must have been when his wife had died.

When Charles learnt that her father had died, he said, "You will always be welcome in my house."

Fiona wasted no time in making a reservation on Aer Lingus. At Gatwick Airport, she heard her name announced on the intercom. When she arrived, the receptionist informed her a man was waiting to see her. A rising sense of apprehension overtook Fiona. Could it be that she didn't want to create a scene at the airport? That's precisely what she would do if Rory McCormack dared to persuade her to marry him. She had too many matters of serious importance on her mind.

Coming towards Fiona as she waited at the intercom desk was none other than Lord Robert Von Pragh. Although she was sick at heart, his presence renewed her spirit. He was looking more handsome than ever and surprisingly relaxed.

"I'm terribly sorry," he said, "to hear about the death of your father. What can I do for you?"

"I'm so upset I don't know whether I'm coming or going."

"That's only natural. I'll give you my number. Call me if any problem arises. Call me anytime, day or night. Do you hear me?"

"Yes." She felt wrapped in a cocoon of delight.

"Where did your father live?"

"In Virginia, America."

"So you're American."

"No. I was born in Ireland. I never knew my mother."

"How sad."

Fiona suppressed a tear welling in her eye.

"God gives us heavy burdens in life," Lord Von Pragh said. "I knew that about you when I met you."

"You did?"

"It's what attracted me to you." His eyes were compelling and magnetic. "Now here you were, going off on your own without telling me."

"It was too painful to talk about my father. He was the kindest man I've ever known. The sun, moon, and stars shone from him as far as I'm concerned."

"What beautiful memories."

"That's all they are. Memories."

Lord Von Pragh was about to speak when he was interrupted by the announcement:

"Passenger for Flight 228 from Gatwick to Shannon Airport will now board at gate 4."

A protective hand pressed her closer to him as Lord Von Pragh kissed Fiona on the cheek, filling her with a sense of power and the knowledge that he could rock her out of her senses and fill her with erotic sensations.

When she had seated herself comfortably in the seat, she thought Lord Von Pragh was like a guardian angel hovering in the wings to comfort and help her.

Reminiscing about her brief relationship with Lord Von Pragh, Fiona realized that she seemed to be in trouble of one kind or another. He had helped alleviate the pain she had felt at the bottom of her heart on the shocking sudden news. She wondered how she would survive without him.

Was she becoming too dependent on Lord Von Pragh? Fiona asked. Was she making a nuisance with one tribulation after another? Why couldn't she be like a normal person with less problems? It seemed no length of time before the plane landed at Shannon Airport.

Fiona had no idea of train and bus schedules. She was in a dilemma about where to start getting transportation to Tipperary. Even though it was only a matter of thirty miles, it might be some time before a bus would depart.

A young woman in green uniform appeared and said, "Ms. Fiona?"

"Yes."

"You're car is waiting for you."

She escorted Fiona outside to the curb.

A stocky man got out of the limousine and said, "Ms. Morgan, where's your luggage?"

"I have none."

"We'll be on our way then. Mr. Dwyer put the car at your disposal."

"That's very nice of him. I was wondering how I'd get there."

"Thomas Dwyer is a good man. His brother puts the bejeesus in me."

"That's interesting."

"I hope they're not related to you."

"To be honest, I've never met them."

"Oh! I thought they were family."

"No."

Fiona was exhausted and sat back in the grey upholstered limousine. At times she was nodding off to sleep. She didn't know whether it was the excitement of seeing Lord Von Pragh or the tumult that had occurred in her life.

In some ways, Fiona realized she was an escape artist. When situations bogged her down, she would go to sleep. She knew it wasn't like this for everybody, but it was her way of coping with stress. She was barely aware of the farmhouses and boreens she passed.

Everything was the same except there was no livestock fare. For that, Fiona was grateful as the limousine passed the Rock of Gusleck, where Lord Von Pragh's wife lay in a vault. She thought of the dramatic change that seemed to have taken place since the night she had met him in the castle.

Did Lord Von Pragh now feel guilty since he had left his deceased wife? Fiona knew it to be a healthy sign for him to be socializing once more. She missed him very much but was insistent on doing things right by herself.

The driver drove the limousine through the great winding curve to the offices of Dwyer and Dwyer, Esq. The male secretary appraised her in awe and then led the way into the dark-paneled office. Both lawyers rose to greet her.

Thomas Dwyer extended his hand and, with her hand cupped in his, said, "It's a pleasure to meet you, Ms. Morgan."

"It's nice to meet you," Fiona replied.

"Do you wish to be called Fiona or Ms. Morgan?"

"Fiona's fine."

"I'm very sorry about your father's death. We'll try to make the transition as easy as possible for you."

"I appreciate that."

"Our law office is handling his will through the American law office of Cooper and Lily."

"I don't know them."

"Anything you wish us to do on your behalf, we'll be only too happy to oblige. All this responsibility is a lot for one pair of shoulders to handle. We're waiting for your sister to arrive in Dublin from America."

Fiona's eyes widened in astonishment. "I didn't know," she said, "that I've a sister."

"Oh yes," Thomas Dwyer said. "I hear she's a very striking-looking young lady, as good-looking as yourself."

"Yes," Michael Dwyer concurred.

Thomas Dwyer sat back in a large high-backed dark-brown leather chair behind a highly polished oak desk with his fingers intertwined. He was a distinctly handsome man, about five feet eleven inches, approximately fifty years of age with a paunch discreetly hidden by a tailored grey suit and vest. His darting, if not suspicious, grey-blue penetrating eyes seemed to be appraising Fiona. She shifted in her seat.

"Only in death, Fiona, do we learn many secrets. Although you never knew it, you have a sister."

"That's good. I'm not alone."

Yet something uneasy lurked at the back of her mind. As she said the words, she knew she was lying to herself.

Thomas Dwyer continued, "Fiona, I understand your father was an eccentric self-made multimillionaire. There are many in America. Your father dragged himself up by his bootstraps from a warehouse man to become founder, chairman, and CEO of Richmond Tobacco Co. Sit back. Relax. I think you could do with a little sip of Louis XIII brandy."

He arose from the chair and, with a slouching gait, walked to the tall oak cabinet. He pulled up two flaps and several sparkling Waterford glasses automatically rose to the surface. He poured a small amount of Louis XIII into a baccarat crystal glass.

"There," he said. "Take a sip to fortify yourself."

Fiona did his bidding and sipped the drink slowly. She was not going to be able to deal with more bad news. Fiona had never tasted brandy like this, but it certainly warmed her innards.

Thomas Dwyer looked kindly at Fiona and said, "Mr. Frederick Morgan, your father, had been married six times."

"What!" She clutched the crystal to her chest. "Six times. I can't believe that about . . . my . . . father. I never saw with a woman. When we were together, it was always just . . . the two of us." Fiona started to weep uncontrollably.

"Here are some tissues." He took some out of a high gold box and gave them to her.

Fiona wiped her eyes, thinking of Lord Von Pragh. What was he going to think of her?

"Are you prepared for more?" Thomas Dwyer enquired. "I know this is very hard on you."

"It is. I can't bear you defaming his name."

"I would not wish to cause you any pain, Fiona."

"You are."

"Even the nuns at the Ursuline boarding school were unaware that he's been married six times. Thank goodness. They may have regarded you in a different light. To give him his due—and believe me, he's a man you can be very proud of—he was unlucky in love."

"Who were all these women?"

"Six showgirls one after another. He had a penchant for dancers and singers, women on the wild side, you might say. Unfortunately, he divorced all of them, settling a small fortune on each and every one of them. He was no fool though when it came to money. Each of them signed a prenuptial agreement, which was almost unheard of, allowing a million dollars and not a penny more when he left them. He was, I think, more sinned against than sinned, but that's neither here nor there."

"Which one of them was my mother?"

"I told you he was no fool. None of them is your mother."

"Who is my mother?" Fiona was feeling bolder.

"Your mother is a very nice woman."

"Who is she?" she asked, impatience betraying her.

"She's a registered nurse. When your father was in the hospital with emphysema, he was very fond of this nurse who was taking care of him. You must remember that after so many marriages, he distrusted women."

"I can understand that."

"When he was in the hospital, he thought he was going to kick the bucket. He was on prednisone and oxygen. When he got better, he sneaked out of the hospital and made love to the nurse for a sum of money."

"What are you saying? I wasn't even born out of love. I'm illegitimate."

"Mr. Morgan and the nurse did not marry. He chose her because he felt she was a beautiful, respectable woman with solid, down-to-earth qualities, which underneath he basically admired. She was engaged to another man at that time. He paid her handsomely to have you so that you would be the sole heir to his vast fortune."

"Where did this happen?"

"He met her in Doctor's Hospital in New York City. You were conceived in a suite, which he maintained at the Carlyle Hotel. His chauffeur and confidant helped him to arrange everything, even though he was quite sick."

"Where's my mother now?"

"Married in America to some man. Your father wanted the best for you. He did not want the six wives quibbling and squabbling over his money when he died. I understand you were an angel in his eyes."

"This is all so hard."

"Of course, it is. But you'd have found out sooner or later. His comings and goings were always in the social column. Your birth was kept a big secret. He wanted to surprise them all when he died."

"I'm shocked too. I needn't tell you."

"Whatever his reason for secrecy, he worked hard and played hard. He was an admirable man from the point of view he had virtually no money. He gradually built up the business piece by piece till it became a multimillion-dollar corporation. Other companies tried to buy him out, but he clung to it tenaciously with the fierceness of a justly proud man outmaneuvering every possible takeover candidate. His enemies were many, but none could match him in sheer brilliance. He kept it in the family for you and your sister."

"Why didn't he tell me about my sister?"

"I understand he was a secretive man. He trusted one person, his chauffeur, who acted as friend, confidant, bodyguard, secretary. He was suspicious to a degree about people. The doctor at one point had tried to declare him insane. He fired him and got another."

"My father was never insane. He always had his wits about him."

"Hmm. I can't say. I'm not a psychiatrist."

"I know."

"It was always the ex-wives after him for more money, cost of living expenses and inflation adjustment. They thought they'd squeeze the last dollar out of him, but he was as sharp as a tack. Not for one minute could anyone gyp him. So he became suspicious. So would I if I had been in his shoes. He had the last laugh on all of them from the grave when they find out he has two living healthy children."

"Who is my sister's mother?"

The barrister was silent for several minutes as if he hadn't heard Fiona's question.

"Who's my sister's mother?" she repeated.

"Oh! An American dancer."

"We'll be meeting soon."

"Yes. I've ordered a limousine for her from Dublin airport. It'll be deducted as an expense."

"My father kept a secret life."

"No. The firm tells me that it made news in the social column every time he married. One marriage, to be honest, is enough for me."

The other brother quipped, "Marriage is an unnatural state. How can two strangers live together in peace and harmony? It should be like an insurance policy. If matters are going well, renew it. If not, don't renew it."

Fiona heard the outside doorbell ring. She stiffened as the two lawyers excused themselves. They left Fiona sitting alone for what seemed an eternity, although in actual fact, it was only five minutes. This was a time full of anticipation, and at the same time an uneasy feeling permeated Fiona.

The lawyers ushered a thirtyish woman into the office, who smiled sweetly at Fiona.

"This is your sister, Fiona," one of the Dwyer barristers said. "I'm sure the two of you will want to share some time together."

Fiona shook her warm, clammy hand and said, "I've always wanted a sister."

"So did I. I'm glad at last we've been brought together even if it's by tragic circumstances. Daddy will be missed."

Fiona was silent. It seemed unnatural to hear a stranger refer to her father as Daddy. He was always Fiona's Daddy, and in some inexplicable way, she resented this woman. It wasn't her appearance—dark haired and brown eyes with a pleasingly plump round face. Her nose was hawkish, giving her a patrician look. Extremely well dressed, she wore fashionable accessories. Her jewelry was simple and elegant.

Fiona did not immediately feel a kinship to this stranger as she thought she would. Given time, though, she might change her mind. Fiona observed that when she smiled, her eyes didn't. There was a cold, calculating look about her eyes. Fiona was entitled to her opinion as the two barristers reentered the room.

"Have you two young ladies gotten to know each other a bit?" Thomas Dwyer enquired.

"We haven't learnt that much about one another as we'd like," Tricia said.

Reseated, the barristers cast wary glances towards Tricia. Was that Fiona's imagination, or was it that advised her to use caution?

Thomas Dwyer said, "We've no time to waste. There's a lot to be accomplished before the day is done."

Tricia grasped Fiona's hand. Was it a hand of comfort and friendship? she wondered. Fiona was not used to outward displays of emotion, and neither was her father for that matter. Fiona felt like pulling her hand away but thought it wise not to do so.

Thomas Dwyer said, "As executor of your father's estate, Mr. Frederick Morgan leaves both of you his entire fortune. It is estimated to be seventy million dollars. It shall be divided fifty-fifty between you, leaving each of you thirty-five million dollars. This includes his entire net worth. In the event either of you dies, the entire fortune goes to the surviving party."

Fiona gasped while Tricia hurt her hand as she dug her nails so deeply. This was unbelievable. Fiona wrenched her hand away. Her father had left no money to anybody else.

"I don't know how I'm going to handle all this money," Fiona said. "I didn't realize my father had that type of money."

"That's the secret side of Mr. Frederick Morgan," Thomas Dwyer said. "God rest his soul. He never trusted people."

Tricia said, "I don't take after Daddy in that regard."

With a reproachful look, Thomas Dwyer silenced her. Fiona realized there was something intimidating about these lawyers. Maybe it was the businesslike comments they made about her father. She reminded herself that their job was not an easy one, and she should bear this in mind. Having had no previous dealings with lawyers, she couldn't make a comparison. Fiona heard her sister sniffling.

Then Tricia turned to Fiona, threw her face against her shoulder, and said, "Oh! I miss Daddy."

Both were in tears, consoling each other.

Thomas Dwyer continued, "You will both need someone reliable to manage that money. I'm always available for advice.'

The lawyers rose and shook their hands.

Fiona said, "Tricia, we should go somewhere and get acquainted."

Tricia said, "I'm sorry. The limo is waiting to get me back to the airport to catch the next flight to America. Things are quite hectic because of Daddy's death."

"I understand."

"We'll be in touch."

She left the room, waving good-bye to Fiona.

Thomas Dwyer put a limousine at Fiona's disposal to take her back to Shannon airport. Her mind in a quandary, she said very little to the driver. Frederick Morgan had come and gone with little time for Fiona to grieve. The one man who had meant everything in life was buried probably without fanfare, and not even his beloved Fiona at his gravesite. She had wanted to go to the funeral, but she was not even sure of the town of burial. It all seemed so unnatural.

Fiona's father had taken care of her in life and in death. What had she done for him? Guilt feelings were prodding. Rightly so, she insisted. Even if she were not physically present, she was there in spirit. She comforted herself with the reminder that his suffering had ceased. Feeling in a daze, she boarded the flight back to London.

It was the gloaming hour in London, with people going about their business as usual. No longer did Fiona feel the same. The first time, she had arrived as a virtual pauper. Now she was a multimillionaire with money to do as she pleased. She was impatient to see Lord Von Pragh as she entered Mr. Phelps's house. Quietly she went to her room with Dubois following her.

Somehow Fiona sensed that life would be different. She had the wherewithal to do as she pleased. It was time to start singing lessons and get started on an opera career. She didn't want Lord Von Pragh to consider her no more than a wealthy ne'er-do-well. From an early age, it had been drilled into her head that she must prove a credit to the Ursuline Convent. It was there she had heard stories about women who graduated and winding up with unsavory characters and male fortune hunters who lured women into marriage to leave them alone and penniless.

It was not going to happen to Fiona. Besides, she didn't have any cares in regard to that matter with Lord Von Pragh. He was who he was. With this money, she must get him the best professional treatment in an attempt to restore his sight.

More than anything else in the world, he deserved it, if for no other reason than that he was a wonderful soul. But more so because he had been kind to Fiona at a time when she needed help.

After she had undressed and was in bed, Fiona missed her father more than ever. Then she reminded herself that she should have expected this. He had been in poor health for some time. Then her grandmother's apparition in Bedford Castle came back to her. Yes, she had been right about going to London. It was beyond Fiona's wildest dream to be in such a gay city with the man she loved.

When Fiona met Lord Von Pragh again, she had so much to tell him. Best of all, she wasn't hampered by lack of money to help him. That was assuming he allowed her. At times he could be difficult, but then she made excuses for him. He aroused such depths of yearning and longing that she felt ashamed of herself. Lord Von Pragh was the only person who could swaddle her in joy amongst so much tumult and turbulence.

Although she wanted to deny it, Fiona was delighted that Tricia had returned to America. She was quite capable of taking Lord Von Pragh from Fiona with her good looks and natural sophistication. Compared to Tricia, Fiona was a country hick incapable of making a decision for herself.

Fiona felt inadequate. Tricia would be likely to lure Lord Von Pragh away from Fiona. She would know the numerous techniques of lovemaking, which were foreign to Fiona. She wouldn't have the guilt feeling that Fiona experienced when he merely kissed her. Her whole body yearned for him, causing her to relinquish her Catholic upbringing and suppress desires heretofore unknown to Fiona. And she was not the only competition to Fiona. London was awash with beautiful women capable of snatching Lord Von Pragh away from Fiona.

What about the young socialites in Ischia, clamoring for an eligible husband? Then on the other hand, they might not want to be burdened by a blind man who needed help, although in many ways, he was quite capable of surviving on his own. Or was he?

Of this, Fiona was sure. Lord Von Pragh had soul-searching emotions that could not be altered. Yes, in many ways, he felt sorry for himself. Fiona realized that she had been instrumental in making him travel to London and Ischia, something he had not done for two years.

CHAPTER 12

Determined not to fritter her life away, Fiona ambled to a boutique on King's Row and bought a new woolen dress. It was melon colored with a scalloped hem. It had a matching jacket with a navy silk collar, which made her skin look glowing and paler in contrast. Some hours earlier, she had called the cathedral, inquiring if they needed a singer for Mass.

"You couldn't have called at a better time," the receptionist said. "God answered my prayer. Be here at five o'clock."

Fiona was exultant that she'd have the opportunity to sing in St. James Cathedral. Not only was it a very old Cathedral, but it was capable of accommodating a great number of people. Exposure to a wide audience was what she needed to start a singing career. She was surprised to learn that several men and women were auditioning to be in the choir.

Each candidate was asked to step forward one by one. Fiona was apprehensive about the competition. Most of the applicants had above-average singing voices. Fiona moved to the center of the floor. There was a babble of voices.

Fiona took three deep breaths. The natural sweet quality of her voice caused the other voices to die down as she commanded attention with the rendition of the "Agnus Dei." She felt totally at ease and oblivious to others in the choir loft. Fiona received no indication to stop singing.

At the completion of the hymn, the choir master enquired, "Where did you learn to sing like that, Ms Morgan?"

"At the Ursuline Convent."

"You're talented, no question about it. You sang without once going off-key. Not once. The trouble is, with talented people, someone either steals you away or you go on to become a pop star."

"That's not likely now."

"I know talent when I hear it. Never give up on your singing."

"No. I won't." There was emphasis in her voice.

"Was any member of your family in the music business?"

"I don't think so."

"Can you stay for practice?"

Without hemming or hawing, she said, "Yes."

Two more singers were chosen from the fifteen applicants.

"Hail, rain, or shine," the choir master said, "you must be here three times a week at seven o'clock in the evening."

It gratified Fiona that she would be doing what she loved. It wasn't often that one was given the distinct opportunity to praise the Lord in song while perfecting her art in one of the largest Roman Catholic churches in London. For that she was truly grateful. She would not be paid, but the exposure and practice were worth their weight in gold.

Fiona thought of Lord Von Pragh and how fantastic it was to visualize herself walking down the aisle of the church to the ethereal strains of the "Hallelujah" chorus.

The words were so uplifting, and as she sang, she felt exultant.

Fiona wandered slowly home in the company of a male and female choir members. They stopped for several minutes outside Fiona's residence, talking about singing and their aspirations.

Fiona thought she saw a bright light go on in the sitting room whereas before it had been lit by a low-wattage corner lamp. Charles bid her good night and left her alone with Lord Von Pragh.

The latter kissed her softly on the cheek, causing her heart to go pitter-patter. He led her to the couch.

"I was thinking of you," he said, "all the time while you were away. What have you done? Bewitched me with that Celtic voice and face?"

"I hope so," she said with an impish grin.

"It's no laughing matter. I can't get you out of my mind when you're away from me. I want to penetrate your mind, body, and soul."

Were these the lines he had oft repeated to Christiana and those who had preceded her?

He grabbed her with such a ferocity that made her body limp. There was a long pause.

"I think of you too," she said, probing his eyes for the truth.

"You do. Why didn't you call me when you returned from Ireland?"

"I had to go to church for an audition."

"Yes. I forgot that you have a life of your own."

"You have a life too."

"Even though I was at London's Art Society Club, surrounded by beautiful women, not one of them could compare to you."

Fiona felt a twinge of jealousy, which she was not going to show Lord Von Pragh.

After several minutes of silence, she said, "I wish I'd been with you."

"I don't want to hamper your lifestyle. That's not why you came to London."

"My career is important. So are you."

"The event I attended wasn't merely social. Before the party, I met a genius from America who fascinated me. He invented this magic show for children and young adults with puppets and muppets with such outlandish stories that actually have meaning. The costumes are bright, gay, and funny. He's the creator of this show. He worked on it for years. Nobody will give him a chance to broadcast his animation series."

"Why not?"

"Money's tight all over today. Nobody's willing to hedge their bets on it."

"I suppose it could be dicey."

"Lord Soames and I watched it. I felt I was a child again without a cane or a care in the word. We laughed our heads off." He intertwined his finger in her, causing such rapturous tingling.

Fiona continued, "Television has a knack of getting one out of a rut. Children need all the help they can get. I believe it broadens their imagination."

"I bet you're imaginative in bed."

"Why? Are you hung like a . . . bull?"

He threw his cane aside and roared with laughter. After some minutes, the laughter subsided. With both hands, he drew her face to him gently. Kissing her on her closed eye, he scrolled down her cheek with his hot tongue, sending waves of rapture through her thighs.

"This must not be," she told herself.

He was flicking his tongue in and out of her mouth, which was slightly ajar, and she succumbed to sensations that were not of this earthly world. Why oh why must she be a slave to the pleasures of the flesh? She had to admit she was. His tongue moved in and out with such deliberate sensation that she wanted and pleaded within herself to move away.

No. Fiona was trapped like an imprisoned slave. Her body, pliant, soft, and supple, she felt he could do anything to her and she would not be able to resist. But resist she must. And yet her body sought him with an urgency and fervor that she instinctively knew must be mutual. Sensible thinking was out of the question.

Who needed sense in this glorious, wondrous moment? Not Fiona. And by the looks of things, neither did Lord Von Pragh. With the urgency of a fire alarm, he pressed his body against her so that she thought that he was in her. But no, he was not. Fully clothed, he breathed deeply and heavily so that Fiona thought he would consume her. Then it happened. That cold wafting air permeated the couch and living room. Yes, it was Christiana interfering at the most inopportune time. No. It was not the wind. It was not the slightly ajar door.

It was the presence of Christiana, jealous and feverish in her quest to pull Fiona away from Lord Von Pragh. Was Fiona deluding herself? In such an ecstatic state, it was quite possible she was. But love made no sense.

Was it love or merely succumbing to the passionate embraces of a man who had been loveless and lonely for too long? His penis was erect, and he was fumbling for the zipper. He held her hand tenderly. Was that her imagination, or did Fiona hear something outside the door? He pulled the zipper down, when Fiona heard the soft steps of someone. Stopped in her tracks, she saw the wagging tail of Dubois, the terrier.

Exasperated, she said, "Go away."

Dubois leapt forward through the door and barked so that he was impossible to resist. A fierce resentment arose within Fiona. This was not the terrier's doing. It was Christiana, and Dubois was under her spell. He ran back and forth frantically. Why did he have to choose such an inopportune time? He ran to the door, humping on it so that he wouldn't have a mishap in the house. Fiona excused herself from Lord Von Pragh. He seemed testy and irritable.

As she hurried though the door, Lord Von Pragh said, "I'll be waiting for you."

With Dubois leading the way, Fiona went outside to the sidewalk partly in a daze and not too pleased with the current circumstances. Who was she to blame? Lord Von Pragh for literally tearing at her heart strings or still communicating with a dead wife who controlled him? She was betwixt and between in this dilemma. Whose dilemma was it? Lord Von Pragh's or Fiona's? Christiana was dead and dead for evermore; she could not place the blame on Lord Von Pragh. What was the point? There seemed to be no solution. Thinking that there would be a volcanic explosion, Christiana showed no mercy. Wasn't mercy and compassion to be expected from the dead?

Fiona wondered if Christiana had been a kind lady in the living. Time and time again she had made an appearance, causing Fiona to doubt whether Lord Von Pragh had severed the bond between them. The only conclusion she could reach was that he was a prisoner of love.

Fiona must forge ahead on her own. Being led by a blind man into thinking she was in love could bring nothing but sorrow. Returning to the, house Lord Von Pragh patted the couch, indicating he wanted her to sit beside him.

"To get back to what we were discussing," he said, "this show was so enthralling that Lord Soames and I are willing to put up money to invest in it to put it on the air."

"It could be, I suppose, a huge hit or flop."

Gone were all his thoughts of lovemaking. Fiona must not dwell on this. Whatever made him happy was foremost in her mind.

"Maybe you've a talent like this American genius, Fiona. He has an incredibly childlike mind. We're willing to back him up one hundred per cent."

"The arts can take us into a world that seems to put one in touch with a higher being. I didn't tell you I'm going to study meditation and Reiki healing."

"You'll be studying so much I'll never be able to see you."

"You can't see me now."

"I have a vivid imagination and can visualize what you look like even though I'm blind. At least you have some substance. These women at the party were just that to me. Party girls. You know what happens to most party girls. Eventually, they get tired of the merry-go-round, and boredom sets in. I never want to be bored with you."

"You're an enigma to me."

"You aren't the first to tell me that."

"I want you to come to church on Sunday and listen to me sing. I want you to listen carefully, and hear my voice through the choir. Will you?"

"I want you to know that you're the first person who lured me back into the church since Christiana died. I was a member of the Church of England."

"Am I the only privileged person?"

"You might say so. We've a date in church. I wish it were in bed. I hope it won't be our last."

Fiona was exultant when he uttered those words. Was he developing a stronger bond with her? Her imagination was not wild enough to visualize the heights of sexual freedom she could attain with him. Could he soar her to realms of ecstasy that heretofore she had not known? And why not? Both lonely and uninvolved, they could achieve heights of lust certainly forbidden by the Ursuline nuns. But what care she at this moment? With hormones raging, she wanted him desperately, passionately, and forever. She wanted him to be the exclusive one. How could she achieve that? He mesmerized her for reasons that she could not explain.

This was a man she must not let slip through her fingers. Could Fiona satisfy Lord Von Pragh? More than anything in life, the answer was an unequivocal yes. He could transport her to heights that were not of this world. Forget the Catholic upbringing. Why must she feel guilty about entering worlds of sinful pleasure? After all, the senses were meant to be enjoyed to the fullest. Wasn't Lord Von Pragh entitled to have a life of hedonistic pleasures? Or was he?

Hypersexuality was known to accompany psychic blindness. Yet a fierce unease disturbed Fiona. What kind of woman would Lord Von Pragh think Fiona was with a self-made multimillionaire father who had tied the knot six times? Her father could have made a mistake once, but five more times. How was she going to relate the story of a father who paid a nurse to conceive Fiona so that he had an heir? Then he had paid Fiona's mother not to have any further dealings with his daughter. His background sounded more sordid than that of a gangster. It was worse. Most gangsters had family values. Their children were shielded from the seamy side of life.

Yet Fiona's father had protected her adequately by sending her to a respectable horse-training community where she could grow up with decent, average, hardworking people. This was a place where horse owners sent their horses for elite training to compete in the Kentucky Derby, Belmont and international competitions. This was the crux of the matter. Lord Von Pragh was not an average person. As a member of the House of Parliament, he had full sway in the running and enactment of the laws of England.

CHAPTER 13

Fiona had to be up early on Sunday morning for the High Mass. She took her place in the choir loft. How religious Lord Von Pragh was was a mystery to Fiona. From his conversation, she had gathered that he had become antireligious since the sudden death of his wife. She regarded that as a normal reaction of an angry man. She was not about to persuade him one way or another to attend church. All she knew is that she would like him to hear her sing and get his honest opinion. Honest he was if nothing else could be said about him.

Fiona and the members of the choir sang to the accompaniment of the organ. Till Communion time, Fiona would have no idea how many people attended church. Because London was predominantly Protestant, she did not expect many parishioners. Situated in the working class section of Paddington, the church was badly in need of repairs. The high dome definitely needed a paint job. There was paint peeling in sections. Some of the pews were so old that the wood was splintered. The priest urged the congregation at collection time to donate extra money for the repairs. Fiona had no idea whether it fell on deaf ears or the congregation was moved to generosity.

Whether Lord Von Pragh was in attendance was Fiona's main concern. After the priest had swung the censer, the smell of incense emanated throughout the church. The soloist sat down, holding her head. The choir master directed Fiona to take over her job of singing the "Magnificat." Fiona felt her voice was not that good in the morning. But she did her best in heavenly music under the circumstances while the soloist was assisted outside to the brisk fresh air.

LOVE THAT NEVER DIES

At the conclusion of Mass, Fiona descended the rickety choir loft staircase, wondering about the condition of the soloist. She would see to it that she got home safely. The choir master informed her that the sick soloist had been driven home. Lord Von Pragh approached her from the thin gathering.

"Fiona." He kissed her on the cheek, sending waves of rapture through her body.

"Robert," she said in an anguished tone of voice, "I didn't really expect you to come."

"I've been an atheist since Christiana died. You might bring me back into the fold."

"There are worse things you could do. I think we all need a respite from the gaiety of London."

"Don't be offended when I tell you this. Your rendition of the 'Magnificat' was so moving. It brought a tear to my eyes that I almost ran from the church. All I could think of was the same music was played on the day of my marriage, not I can say, with the majesty of your voice."

Fiona sighed and, in a breathless voice, said, "Thank goodness you like it. It's a bit of a strain early in the morning. I sing better later on. I'm more of a night owl."

"I know of a better thing to do at night, but let that be a prelude of better things to come."

"If you can do better than that, my hat goes off to you." He bowed. "You're wasting your talent by doing anything other than singing."

"I love it very much."

"It's easy to tell. You're a natural-born singer."

"Thank you." She smiled an impish smile.

"That's all the more reason you must follow your dreams. When you get to be as old as I am and beset with blindness, you'll regret it if you do not."

"The choir master gives me good cues and prompts."

"He cannot put the emotion and gut-wrenching pathos you convey. You inspire love and tenderness with your voice. I haven't seen the hot, temperamental side of you, which is probably lurking somewhere within."

"I sing from the heart."

"If every artist and would-be artist did that, it'd be such a beautiful world."

Fiona and Lord Von Pragh walked down hand in hand through the short lawn with bluebells and daffodils peeping through the short grass. They passed a graveyard where bouquets and flowers were laid at the base of many tombstones. She thought it in the best interest of Lord Von Pragh not to mention it.

Further along at the next corner, everything was hurly-burly with men shouting from atop wooden butter boxes, each one spouting his own ideals. From time to time, their voices were drowned out by honking cars and passengers that impeded traffic.

They went into a Kardomah café, within shouting distance of the idealistic individuals. He ordered a cappuccino.

"Radicals," said Lord Von Pragh, "have a definite place in our society. I like to know what they're griping about. I was as radical as any of them when I attended Cambridge."

"I suppose they have a point."

"Sometimes they have legitimate views. If it weren't for the few who risk mistreatment, stone throwing, and possibly jeering, their causes would never come to light. Often they have a huge silent following, but it's these demonstrators who risk their lives."

"There must be more peaceful methods of attaining goals."

"Tell me whoever brought about drastic change by peaceful measures?"

"Offhand, I can't remember." She sipped the cream-laden cappuccino.

"You can't remember, Fiona, there aren't many. Peace is for the dead. Fighting is for the living. People have fought for honor, love, be it a man or a woman, for country, for religion, money, food, whenever they feel threatened."

"Why don't you fight to restore your sight?"

"Bravo! I'm glad to hear you say that. You know who put me in that frame of mind, Fiona? You."

"I'm glad."

"You've got the gumption to do it. I want to see your beautiful face that must go with such a melodious voice."

"I don't guarantee that."

"Even if your face weren't beautiful, if it were scarred or not what society considers asymmetrical and lovely, I should still love you. A voice can have a profound effect on me. I'm so sensitive to a voice that I can almost hear a pin drop."

"That's a mighty burden."

"It depends. I wouldn't want to listen to the screams and harping of a shrew. It would make something die in me."

"Well, of course, you have to listen to a voice during waking hours."

"Your voice, Fiona, is my eyes."

"I know a little about voice vibration."

"Yes."

"First you sit in a comfortable position. After taking deep breaths in an out, you call on your spirit guide."

"Who is that?"

"It could be an angel. It could be the spirit of someone who was very close to you in life and has passed over to the other side."

Fiona felt a cold sensation between her and Lord Von Pragh. The mere mention of the spirit realm had precipitated the presence of Christiana. While Fiona was disturbed by the entity, Lord Von Pragh continued sipping cappuccino. Fiona decided to let Christiana disturb her. In a sense, she accepted the situation. It dawned on her that his deceased wife could be useful.

Fiona said, "I know that with repetition of *om* for as long as possible, one enters another dimension during meditation into the alpha state. The senses are heightened that one can perceive other realms. One can bring about a dramatic healing effect."

"Hmm. I've other important things on my mind, such as making love to you."

Ignoring his remarks about love, she said, "Don't scoff at it."

"I'm listening, Fiona."

"You can channel across thousands of miles, meet your spirit guides who will identify themselves. This applies specifically to you, Robert. You can heal yourself or another person."

"If I sat in my flat, chanting the same sound for twenty minutes or more, I'm sure I'd be carted off by the white-coated men as someone who had gone soft in the head."

"Don't be so cynical about something you've never tried. You can do it with soft meditation music in the background."

"Doesn't it put you to sleep?"

"It definitely relaxes. There's no need to sleep. If anything, you should be wide awake and entranced by seeing images you couldn't normally see with the naked eye."

"But I can't see."

"That's it. You don't have to see. You'd enter a world where ordinary mortals can't enter. You could ask God or your angel to restore your sight."

"If that's the case, why aren't millions of people doing it to improve their lives?"

"That's the point. Monks, Buddhists, gurus, and people with a spiritual inclination are doing it to get in touch with a higher being."

"How long do you do it, Fiona?"

"Twenty minutes is enough."

"You're telling me I can restore my sight and become a useful member of society."

"Yes."

"You live in another world. If I could do that, I'd have done it when the affliction started."

"The longer you do it, the deeper you get in touch with your higher self. Mystics have been doing it for centuries. People in the arts and creative endeavors are attracted to it, as it opens up a whole new world that they never believed existed. Not only that, but you, Robert, can actually feel and see for yourself areas of the body that need to be healed."

"This is England, Fiona, not Celtic Ireland. I know of absolutely no one who does this. Meditation, yes, but chanting *om* over and over again, no."

"People don't know what they're missing."

"I'm afraid I don't want to know." He wiped his eyes.

"You could get in touch with your spirit guides who invariably have some function in life."

"As I know virtually little about the subject, I won't argue with you, dear spiritual Fiona."

"The more I practice, the more attuned I become. My voice even seems better."

"That is only if you believe in it."

"I do."

"I wasn't asking you to marry me. I like the way you say 'I do.'"

"You do, do you?"

Fiona wanted and needed Lord Von Pragh. She must have him. She wanted to kiss him, hug him, hold him so that he never wanted to let her go. She wanted to reach heights of pleasure with him that Christiana had. Yet she thought realistically that she must be crazy. She wanted him to be in her, feel her, touch her so that she reached nirvana. Was she asking too much? Did she want to face the same fate as the unfortunate woman who took her own life when Lord Von Pragh rejected her?

But that was the crux of the matter. Love is blind, blind as a bat and unable to see reality. Determined to fill the void that had been absent in Lord Von Pragh's life for too long, she resolved to get at the bottom of the matter. Who could Fiona believe? The lawyer or Lord Von Pragh?

Maybe Fiona was naïve. However, her belief in Lord Von Pragh never wavered. He was the epitome of what every woman desired. Did the lawyer have his own interest at heart? Quite possibly. Never had she thought this about Lord Von Pragh. So what if he wanted her in bed? She had to admit that she yearned for him more, more than Christiana or the hapless woman who took her own life.

Lord Von Pragh aroused in Fiona depths of passion that she knew instinctively he must be the one for her. Yet she had no experience in dealing with such a worldly man. She was a slave, and there was no other way of fathoming such gut-wrenching emotion that could only be sated by him.

By hook or by crook, Fiona must learn to suppress her desires. Was it possible?

After learning the facts and trying to weigh the decision, she must come to a single conclusion. Right or wrong, she must guard against stupidity. Young and immature, she had to go through a learning process.

Fiona knew that Lord Von Pragh was the man she must be with. If only she had her father around to guide her. Yes. She needed help and had nowhere to turn.

It would thrill her beyond earthly desires to be asked in his timbre voice if she would marry him. The chances were so remote.

"You don't confide in me, Fiona." The voice of Lord Von Pragh was reproachful. "Things that you should tell me, you go and tell Mr. Phelps."

"Yes," she replied, her tone noncommittal.

"Do you think that I'm a fortune hunter?"

"You're my ideal fortune hunter. Please get that out of your head once and for all."

They had almost reached the house.

"Instead of going to your flat in Brompton, why don't we head to mine in Kensington?" he said.

That suggestion pleased Fiona. Dotted along the street were expensive antique stores, stables, and townhouses. They rode the elevator to the sixth floor penthouse. Fiona was aghast at the size of the parlor. At a glance, the contents of the room made it obvious that the man was a world traveller.

Nothing but the best did Lord Von Pragh bestow on Christiana, Fiona thought with a twinge of jealousy. Inside the short hallway leading to the parlor was a hand-carved table, which must have taken a year or more for the craftsman to complete, so intricate was the design of the top and minute details in the legs. There were ivory statues and statuettes on the mantelpiece.

Fiona said, "This penthouse is beautiful. However, if you saw how the elephant calves are left motherless in the wilderness and unable to forage for themselves, you wouldn't buy these priceless pieces of ivory."

"I'm in agreement with you, Fiona. It was given to us as a present by an African prince."

"Thank goodness you're not decimating the elephant population and filling the coffers of the tribesmen."

"They have to live too, Fiona."

"God would not have put the elephants on earth if they didn't serve a function. One or two elephants can replace humans and haul heavy loads that men, the so-called superior beings, are not capable of doing. If we followed their footsteps, we could avoid being drowned when the heavy rains and tsunami hit the earth."

Expensive handmade Persian rugs of varying sizes were strewn on the parquet floor. An antique sword with a sharp edge lay horizontally on the wall, which had belonged to a Roman nobleman. The latter's initials were engraved on the handle. The lighting was low with Turkish lamp shades. A spiked silver coffee pot and Worcestershire china cups and saucers rested on a side table.

The sad, sweet strains in the baroque role in *The Tales of Hoffmann* played hauntingly in the background. Although Christiana had been gone for two years, she seemed to loom large as they ascended the sweeping staircase to the second floor. Inside the room, on the mantelpiece above a wood-burning fireplace, were photographs of Lord Von Pragh and Christiana in a sweet embrace. Leaning against a silent upright Ferrari piano of which there are only five in the world, Fiona examined the photograph carefully, wishing she could fathom what it was that made his deceased wife so special. She noticed that there was a kindly quality of her eyes, but other than that, there was nothing to avow such fathomless fealty.

There were old Dutch paintings on the wall. A Claude Monet painting sat to the right. Trudging slowly, Lord Von Pragh took Fiona's hand to the third floor. A huge double bed adorned the center of the room. White silk curtains billowed softly in the evening breeze. A Bible rested on the table beside the bed. On the other side were numerous photographs of Christiana and Lord Von Pragh in various parts of the world in different poses.

One factor loomed in all the pictures. They looked happy. Oh! How jealous Fiona felt.

Turning to Fiona, Lord Von Pragh said, "I must remind you. You're the first lady to enter this room since the death of my wife."

Lord Von Pragh made himself comfortable in a nearby chair. He pulled closer to Fiona and cupped her hand in his. Waves of glorious feelings permeated Fiona's body that she felt transported to another world.

"I must confess," he said. "I miss Christiana very much."

"I understand." She pressed his strong hand firmly.

There was silence for what seemed an interminable length of time.

"I resolve to turn over a new leaf. I must for your sake. Otherwise, I know I'm going to lose you."

"Do you want that?"

"Certainly not. Let's lie on the bed where I loved and worshipped Christiana." Lord Von Pragh led Fiona to the bed. Silently they lay side by side without uttering a word. Her nostrils inhaled the wonderful scent of cedar as she shared the pillow with him. What a masculine outdoorsy aroma it was. He moved closer to her.

He whispered, "Do you realize what you mean to me to be sitting by my side? That's how much." He pressed his strong, taut muscular body to her.

"I know I have to have a life of my own. If ever there was anybody I would want to share it with, it is you and you only."

"You mean everything to me. You are more than life itself to me." He kissed her fervently on the eyes, down to her lips.

His tongue probed her mouth that she became lost in the glory. She responded voraciously so that she was unable to control her emotions. Yet she thought, why should she restrain herself? This transformation of Lord Von Pragh was something she had not witnessed before and perhaps never again. She must take advantage of this unique opportunity. He pressed her body so close to her that she felt at one with him. He moved down her body. He kissed her breast, arousing such sensations. She parted her legs automatically.

Fiona's body yielded and succumbed to his every move. Lord Von Pragh moved down to her throbbing pubic area. She was so moist that he pressed his tongue on both sides of her inner thighs.

Pulsing with desire for him, she pressed her body urgently to him. Her clitoris was upright, and she savagely thrust it to him. Waves of rapture enveloped her body. Her legs moved wider apart.

"I want you," he whispered. "I need you."

She wanted to thrust her body to him. Grappling between desire and the impulse to control herself, she felt like a volcanic explosion. She knew she could reach nirvana within seconds. Her body squirming, she thrust forward with such a ferocity that she felt ashamed. A swoosh of cold air enveloped the bedroom.

Suddenly it happened. The silk screen near the bed banged on Fiona's legs with such a thud it brought her partly back to reality. She let out a faint cry. But she was pitiless, helpless—pitiless for Christiana, who was interfering again, and helpless to deal with the throbbings he had evoked within her. She vowed she must be better than Christiana. Sense no longer meant any sense. Why must she be so depraved to yield to the longings of the flesh?

It was flesh on flesh, blood on blood, heat on heat coursing through her veins.

How magnificent it felt. Not for a minute did she think it could come crashing down. At this time, she needed no outside interference. Lord Von Pragh was locked between her legs so that she never wanted to let him go. Her thighs squeezed him so tightly that she thought he was a prisoner. Let him be a prisoner. She never wanted to release him. But the pain from the blow increased in intensity.

Rising from the bed, Lord Von Pragh sighed, "It's never ending."

CHAPTER 14

While Fiona had become a multimillionaire, her lifestyle had not changed that dramatically. There were several invitations to the millionaires' club, investment clubs, as well as many requests for charities and funds for one cause or another. She spent a great deal of time dealing with her lawyer in London, who was also her confidant. She moved into her own flat in Brompton, which was comfortable.

However, Fiona became distressed when her trust and estate lawyer said, "I've watched your money grow, Fiona. I don't want you to wind up penniless. It's one of the reasons I take a personal interest in you."

"What news do you have about my sister?"

"None. There never was a sister to my knowledge. I'll get back to that. It's the company you keep, Fiona, that concerns me."

"What do you mean?"

"I'm referring to your paramour, Lord Von Pragh."

"He's a real gent."

"He may be to you. How much do you know about him?"

"Not very much. But he always helped me in many ways."

"It is my understanding that he hasn't two cents to rub together. He put every penny he had into a television venture that'll probably go down the tubes. How is a blind man going to support himself?"

"I'd love him whether he was a pauper or a millionaire."

"I'm your lawyer, Fiona. I have your best interests at heart. I don't want fortune hunters running after you."

"I didn't have a penny when he met me. I can't see that he had any idea about my money."

"A man like Lord Von Pragh has a way of finding these matters out."

"Impossible. I don't believe it for one second."

"I'm your counsel. How is this Lord Von Pragh going to support you or himself?"

"His television venture may take off. I've complete confidence in him. He's no fly-by-night."

"Television is risky. Any man with a brain in his head wouldn't risk what he's risked."

"I love him."

"You love him," he said, exasperation in his voice. "I'm much older than you. You have a lot of time and thinking to do about love. Love a man with social standing and money."

"Lord Von Pragh is a conservative member of Parliament and not without social standing."

"There are a lot of matters, though unconfirmed, that are dicey about him."

"Tell me one."

"He was married. His wife died. That can happen. Suddenly he can't see."

"My heart goes out to Lord Von Pragh. It's obvious he loved his wife dearly."

"He goes to one ophthalmologist after another. Nobody can do anything for him. I tell you he's faking blindness."

"It's real to him. Therefore, he must be considered blind."

The lawyer picked up several sheets of paper stapled together and leafed through them. He said, "I've gained access to copies of bills here from to Harley Street specialists that I feel that he should pay. He'd be better off meeting his obligations instead of putting his money into what may turn out to be a television scam."

"It's true. Nobody has heard of the young artist. But new artists come on the scene without credentials. People like Lord Von Pragh and Lord Soames have the vision to believe in his talents."

Leaning toward Fiona, he said, "There are other matters that are far more serious to be taken into consideration."

"Such as?"

"Before he married, he led a scandalous life bedding women at every opportunity."

"He's not the first man who has done that. He won't be the last either."

"His name was in every tabloid recording his latest conquest like an ongoing soap opera. The lurid details titillated the public. He never stayed with a woman for any length of time. He discarded them at his whim like rags, as if they had no emotion."

"That surprises me."

"This is what galls me, Fiona. His young unfortunate mistress took her own life on the day of his wedding."

Fiona shuddered. "What a tragedy." Shivers of fear made her tremble despite trying to keep a stoic appearance.

"Here's a young woman who could have any man she wanted, and she falls for Von Pragh."

"Was she very beautiful?"

"Too beautiful for her own good. Is it any wonder that the poor despise and distrust the rich and titled?"

"I'm inclined to agree with you."

"I don't want to see the same happen to you. You're not some piece of trash to be discarded at his whim. He's a coldblooded individual. Even the papers who stalked his every move had little sympathy for him when his wife died after two years."

"It almost seems like a law of karma. What he sowed he reaped."

"I'm an atheist, Fiona. There are certain values that must be upheld whether you're titled or not. I don't want to see your name dragged in the mud like your father's. God knows it wasn't his fault."

"You've got me thinking. I never suspected anything like that about Lord Von Pragh."

"No. You wouldn't. I'm trying to protect you. Will you get it into your head?"

"I've no intention of killing myself for any man," she said, a steely determination in her voice.

"I hope not, least of all for that worthless Lord Von Pragh."

"I think he was faithful to his wife."

"He had to keep his nose clean. He was ostracized by certain members of society after the woman's suicide."

"What was his wife like?"

"Plain, wealthy. She kept him on a short leash. Precisely what such a rogue needed."

Matters were beginning to click in Fiona's head She was silent for several minutes.

She said, "If there are any other matters to discuss, I'll be at home in Brompton."

"Good-bye. Don't be blinded by love."

Trying to disguise the hurt that stabbed at her heart Fiona left the law office in a totally different frame of mind. She loved Lord Von Pragh. How could she forget the wondrous, glorious feelings that he had engendered in her? She had been in a place with him that was beyond her wildest imagination. Was this the man destined for her as predicted in the apparition in Bedford Castle by her grandmother? Let it be, she prayed.

Contrary to the lawyer's statement, Fiona still doubted that Lord Von Pragh was a fortune seeker in his relationship with her. She was betwixt and between whether the scandal she had heard about Lord Von Pragh was worth considering. But consider it she must, if she had an ounce of sense.

Money hadn't changed Fiona. Or had it? She'd have to mull over this story. It was preposterous that Lord Von Pragh should desire Fiona for wealth. Wealth had never entered the picture. Yet he had been irked by Fiona not revealing what had transpired in Ireland.

Why had Lord Von Pragh hired lawyers to authenticate the existence of Fiona's sister? It was perplexing. His private life was sordid, and it was a side of him that she had least expected.

Then Fiona reminded herself that life had been full of surprises in such a short length of time. When would they cease? She was disappointed in the man who had meant everything to her, the man who had soared her to realms of height and ecstasy that heretofore she had not known.

How was Fiona going to broach Lord Von Pragh about such a story? Would he take offense and tell her it was none of her business? The life he had led prior to his marriage was strictly his. When it amounted to trampling on a sensitive woman's feelings culminating in suicide it involved Fiona. She trembled at the realization that she could have been in this woman's shoes.

How could Lord Von Pragh be so callous to marry one woman while his mistress lay dead? It outraged Fiona. That was it. She must sever her relationship with him now. No time must be wasted. There was no need for explanation.

CHAPTER 15

Determined that she was not going to be a victim of Lord Von Pragh, Fiona walked to Charles Phelps's house in a contemplative mood. The side of her true friend described by her lawyer was like a stab in the heart. How could a man be so ruthless to marry another while his mistress had committed suicide?

Was Lord Von Pragh more callous and conniving than Fiona had imagined? Did she have blinders on in her friendship with him? Fiona thought of the many times his wife had come between them. Frankly, she was not surprised that Christiana had married him by hook or by crook.

The marriage sounded sordid and could bode no good. The very fact that Lord Von Pragh could smile happily while he put the wedding ring on Christiana's third finger of the left hand was searing at Fiona's heart. Were they really meant for each other in life and in death?

How was Fiona going to confront him with this news? Immediately her heart cried out that she must leave him now for better or for worse. It seemed only the beginning of a relationship that must be severed once and for all. Yet her heart cried out that she must have him. Yes. She must suppress her desires. Fiona wanted and needed Lord Von Pragh.

Fiona was independent now. She would entrust the information to Charles Phelps. It was imperative that she get his opinion of Lord Von Pragh. She would not mince words. He would tell the truth as bluntly as the lawyer. Yet it was hard to conceive Lord Von Pragh in this dark light, a fortune hunter who pursued Fiona and had no visible means of support.

Supporting Lord Von Pragh was not out of the question. The man needed sympathy for the simple reason he could not see and was disadvantaged as far as employment was concerned. Beset by psychic blindness or visual agnosia seemed to be his misfortune in life.

Fiona wasted no time in heading for Charles Phelps's house. Having someone to confide in was of the utmost importance. Feeling dog tired and bone weary, Fiona hung her coat in the closet on arrival. The dog, Dubois, wagged his tail and kissed her like a long-lost friend.

"Charles," Fiona said, "isn't it a pity that humans don't have a dog's mind?"

"Humans are blessed with the ability to think. Dogs have learnt to serve."

"Why can't humans be like dogs?"

"It would make for a dull world if we were to go around barking."

"You don't get the point I'm making. Charles, I have to tell you something."

Charles closed the *London Times*. The rustle of the paper was annoying to Fiona.

"Want to play the field? Is that it?"

"I wish. He has me hooked. You wouldn't believe what I heard about him."

"What can that be?"

"He seems to be man without a conscience."

"Can't say I got that impression of him. No."

"Would you believe that the day he married Christiana his mistress killed herself?"

"These things happen unfortunately sometimes."

"But to go ahead, marry, and celebrate afterwards is unconscionable?"

"We don't know the whole circumstances. I think life has dealt him a few hard knocks."

"It's fitting after the way he treated that poor woman."

"I'm no prude, but a mistress pays the price for being a mistress. A man does not marry a mistress."

"A gentleman would at least provide for her."

"Lord Von Pragh married a fine woman. It's unfortunate that she died so quickly."

"I wonder if she's not still around."

"What do you mean by that?"

"I've often felt her presence when I was with him. It gives me the willies."

"That's probably your imagination."

"It's not. I'm serious."

"I wouldn't pay it that much mind. You're too sensitive. Does he know this?"

"He does. He pretends the same as you. He says I'm imaginative and it is my Celtic blood."

"Why let it even bother you? His wife can't harm you. She's dead. Dead is dead. She can't come back to life."

"I wonder. I do."

Fiona was fully aware that Charles was watching her out of the corner of his eye as he sipped his tea. There was a rueful smile in his eyes. What was it that amused him? Fiona wondered. She was delighted to see him totally at ease with her. What he thought inwardly was another matter.

While Fiona resolved not to see Lord Von Pragh, she couldn't help but wonder what he was doing. Would her resolve be for naught if he appeared on the doorstep? The idea made her heart tremble. She decided she must not let weakness get the better of her. Superhuman strength would be required to make the transition of not seeing him. The notion of weakness and frailty must be banished from her mind. In its place a steely determination must reign.

But Fiona was not made of steel. She was a woman with the weakness of loving Lord Von Pragh. How she wished he was besotted by her. Grim reality in the vision of the dead mistress flashed before her eyes. It was all too clear. Fiona must sever this unwholesome relationship now. There must be no turning back.

Was it possible that Lord Von Pragh was a clairvoyant? He had confided in her that his senses were heightened since the psychic blindness beset him. Could he read her thoughts? Why hadn't he called her for two days? Did he have a premonition or a dream that

Fiona was not going to see him? Not communicating with her for two days had not been his style. Was it another side she had not seen? Knowing that he could rock her out of her senses, he had abandoned her. It would save Fiona time and unnecessary explanation. If only the situation were reversed and he loved her. Why must Fiona succumb to love?

Wasn't she woman enough to please herself and be comfortable on her own?

Despite Lord Von Pragh's blindness, he proved to be an independent person. It was something admirable about him. There was no whining and self-deprecation. He confronted his one in two billion people affliction like a man. Did he have a secret helper in the guise of his deceased wife? Fiona believed it to be in the realm of possibility.

Yet Fiona would have liked to have been privy to his true feelings when memories of his wife haunted him. Did he too feel that Fiona was an outsider and must remain as such? This was all the more reason Fiona felt in a lurch. Was this a game he played?

Fiona was capable of matching his game. How could she be so deceived? She felt young, inexperienced, and vulnerable, not unlike his mistress. The difference was that Fiona had no experience with men, and she realized she was capable of being hurt very deeply.

Fiona wished she didn't have a heart that she wore on her sleeve. Maybe that was the crux of the matter. Did Lord Von Pragh realize all too clearly the depth of her love for him and had taken full advantage of her? She would learn from this lesson. Exposing her true nature had been a major faux pas. Too late. The deed was done. Now she must suffer the consequences.

For the shoddy treatment Lord Von Pragh had meted to his mistress, Fiona wanted to make him suffer. Was he an absolute hedonist who loved only himself? Had it entered his head to call Fiona? Apparently not.

Two, three, and four days went by. During that time, Fiona tried to hide her agitation, which mounted with every passing hour. She tried to conceal her distrust of Lord Von Pragh. Any woman listening to her story would consider Fiona a lunatic. Hadn't she seen the writing on the wall?

It was time to turn her thoughts to something worthwhile. Fiona was becoming increasingly distressed by not hearing from Lord Von Pragh. Should she swallow her pride and call him? Was he feeling as lonely, the same loneliness she was experiencing? How she missed the tender love, the pungent cedar aroma emanating from him, the rapt kisses that had soared her to another realm. She must consider it only a memory. There must be an escape from once beautiful feelings. She needed no other man to take his place.

Resolved that she must forget Lord Von Pragh, Fiona joined a Reiki healing group in Earls Court. She needed healing as much as Lord Von Pragh. He needed it for visual agnosia. Hers was something else: a broken heart. It dawned on her that he may have another paramour. It was she who needed to heal him. His problem was far more insurmountable than hers. It affected every facet of his life. Did he feel worthless and inadequate? Surely he must at times have entertained such notions. Was he blaming himself for his predicament? No cure whatsoever in sight must lead to bouts of depression.

When Fiona arrived at the flat in Earls Court, she was greeted at the door where she had to place her shoes in the corridor "to leave all negative vibrations outside," as the healer said.

A pale, thin, esthetic red-haired male in his fifties in a low-key monotonous tone said, "You were directed here, Fiona, as we and the others. God has a plan for all of us in this place."

Sitting on a white couch, Fiona observed that there were statues of angels all over the walls. The room was sparse and small save for an altar erected against one wall with a marble statue of angel Gabriel, a fat Buddha, and a lifelike man of Eastern persuasion sitting in the lotus position. Indian guides wearing headdress accompanied by a wolf stared back at Fiona. A bouquet of white carnations rested in a tall vase of water on a table.

Lighted white candles flickered sporadically in blue containers. Because of their healing properties, blue and white predominated. Music that Fiona associated with monks, like Gregorian chant, relaxed her.

Suddenly it dawned on Fiona that perhaps she could help Lord Von Pragh even if they were no longer friends. She was jubilant at the prospect.

The healer said, "I lived the worldly life as a feature film director. I was making a lot of money. I travelled all over the world. I was not at peace with myself. Everything I did was to excess: drink, drugs, and sex. I felt I was in the twilight zone. I couldn't even remember the first name of any woman I slept with, let alone her last name. My friends were dying like flies from the excesses. I decided to change my ways. I entered the healing arts, which is far more satisfying than sex, drugs, and rock and roll. Let's start with Fiona. Tell us why you're here."

"So that I can help others. I think there's more to life than traditional medicine."

"Absolutely," replied the healer.

The other participants gave different reasons for their interest in healing. The healer jangled cymbals while the music lulled Fiona almost to sleep.

"Now take several deep breaths in and out," he continued.

Fiona felt a bit lightheaded with the smell of incense permeating the room and the repetitious Eastern music playing softly in the background on a tape recorder. She wished she could attain the depth of spirituality as the Reiki master. She must banish all worldly thoughts, particularly about Lord Von Pragh.

The Reiki master placed a chair in the middle of the room. He aroused Fiona out of her reverie with a light tap on the shoulder. He directed her to sit on the cushioned chair. While she was in an upright position, the Reiki master hovered his hands over her head while intoning prayers. In a semitrance state, Fiona saw a brilliant white light streak across her face. Was that her angel? she wondered.

When the Reiki master had completed opening the chakras of each individual, a bell chimed for several seconds. There was a five-minute recess.

Again, the Reiki master advised Fiona and the group to close their eyes and place their palms upward on their knees so that they would be receptive to the healing. Deep breathing was resumed. All was quiet within and without, save for the seraphic Gregorian chant. Fiona sensed herself inching deeper into the spirit realm.

Like a bolt out of the blue, Fiona saw Lord Von Pragh with Michael, the archangel, on the other side. At this moment, she cast aside her opinion of Lord Von Pragh. The deeper she concentrated on the vision in her mind's eye, the more convinced she was that he could be healed of visual agnosia despite all the Harley Street ophthalmologists' theories that it was not possible. Yes. Fiona was in another world, communing with her guardian angel.

The Reiki master said, "Call on your spirit guides to surround you."

Fiona was pleasantly surprised when after several minutes, she saw a group of guides attired in full-length white garb in a circle. They were not as earthly beings, but she instinctively knew they must be her guides. In the background, the archangel Michael and angel Gabriel were shrouded in white light.

Fiona felt at peace. Gone were the distress and hopelessness about Lord Von Pragh. Replacing it was a tranquility that had eluded her for the past several days. This was so new and wondrous to physically leave the earth plane and to be transported to the spirit realm.

Fiona and the other students held their hands above the healee. She felt her fingers and hands vibrating and pulsing as the healing students followed one another around in a circle, never removing their hands from above the body on a stretcher. Where healing was needed, Fiona felt a heat radiating from the healee.

When Fiona's chance to lie down came, she at first felt stifled by so many hands. Some healers started at her head, another at her chest area, another at the feet and the rest in between. It was simply a matter of minutes before Fiona fell asleep. On awakening, she apologized. But an apology wasn't necessary according to the Reiki master.

Standing on her feet, Fiona felt refreshed, invigorated, and calm. Banished were her worries about Lord Von Pragh. Admittedly, she felt guilty that she was unaware whether he was sick or troubled.

Walking home that evening, after four hours with the Reiki master, Fiona had no regrets. She still wanted to feel the warmth and tenderness of Lord Von Pragh's touch. She wanted to be close to him, to impart the healing qualities that she felt had been bestowed on her. He must see again. He must be rid of his psychic blindness for all time. He must feel like a full-blooded Englishman as he was before the unfortunate condition beset him. Imagine the power she would feel if she could restore his sight. But she was no miracle worker. She was a woman torn between loving and protecting him and rejecting him.

Life was taking on significant meaning for Fiona. Where once she had worried about money and had to borrow, she questioned why she was not doing something for the less fortunate. And who other than Lord Von Pragh, cursed by psychic blindness, he who meant more than life itself to her? He who could soar her to realms of ecstasy that she was sure no other man could. He who merely, by the flicker of his tongue, could lift her to the heavens, not earthly heavens, but heavens beyond the reach of stars. He who transformed her from being a naïve young woman. He who could transport her to earthly delights that were foreign to her. Heaven and earth united when he touched her. It was like balm to a suffering soul.

Knowing that he suffered more, Fiona must be forgiving. Why must she compromise the sultry lovemaking by trying to punish him? She was a victim as he was. Why not enjoy life and throw caution to the wind? Life is short enough, she thought.

Alas! When was she going to see Lord Von Pragh again? He could not see her, so she must seek him out. He was a man torn between a deceased wife and Fiona. Whom would he choose? Deciding to be every bit as good as Christiana, Fiona said a silent prayer that he would favor her. But she knew there was no guarantee that her prayer would be answered. What was she to do?

Why not do something for the less fortunate? Fiona thought. Homeless people, raving, emaciated, and dying of various ailments, huddled in doorways and the underground, seeking shelter from pitiless passersby. Intercepted were probably robbers, blackmailers, and murderers.

Fiona realized it was time to put her mind to more serious business than Lord Von Pragh. Yet she asked herself, hadn't this man endured enough at the hands of an abusive alcoholic father? Shouldn't she extend mercy to him too who needed it particularly when his activities were curtailed by blindness? Must she let rumor and stories of killing his mistress destroy what perhaps could have been a memorable relationship? Deep down inside, she knew he missed her as much as she longed for him.

It was an entertaining thought and not without foundation that Fiona came to the conclusion that she was becoming immersed in other worldly activities. Uppermost in her mind was Lord Von Pragh. Had purpose and clarity abandoned her?

CHAPTER 16

Next morning, the church was quite full. Fiona sang in the choir. In between she listened attentively to the sermon. The priest did not mince words.

"Our sermon today," he said, "concerns the poor, although essentially it involves every person in this country. As your priest and representative of the Catholic Church, we've always supported the poor in whatever way we can. This new poll tax proposal in Parliament will put a terrible hardship on those people who are barely eking out a living. It penalizes the parents and children. It deprives a child of a slice of extra bread and milk. In London we're aware of the many thousands of children where hunger gnaws at their very bones. Poverty enslaves the poor, its bondage that our Tory leadership knows little about. I urge you to write to your elected official. Flood the House of Parliament with letters and phone calls to veto this new poll tax. Each time you do so, you prevent a child from going to bed hungry."

As she was leaving the church, Fiona wandered among the parishioners, hoping to catch a glimpse of Lord Von Pragh. She muffled her coat about her neck to ward off the stiff northeasterly wind from whipping her cheeks. She thought about the sermon.

"Sign up, please, madam, to attend the rally," was the cry from several men and women sitting at tables outside the church. Fiona had no idea if she would be able to fit the rally into her next hectic schedule, but she vowed to give it her best effort with her signature and address.

The proposal of the poll tax was on the tip of people's tongues. Nobody liked it, but as yet, they were doing little about it. Fiona hoped it would not be long before the masses were stirred to action.

However, Fiona was afraid that she might be recognized at the demonstration and someone would tell her whereabouts to the mayor of Limerick. She was convinced that there were Irish people living in England who would be more than happy to see her marry him.

Fiona was not of the same mind. She must keep her wits about her and not put herself in jeopardy. She would inform her lawyer in London about the incident that had happened in Ireland. She realized that nobody knew what kind of rogue this son of a politician was, particularly due to the fact he was living in another country. At least, Mr. Phelps knew the situation. She had phoned him regularly to keep him abreast of the goings-on. It was part of her daily routine.

Friday was the scheduled noonday rally. Fiona's group from the church was scheduled to meet at Marble Arch in the heart of London. Fiona had taken painstaking delight in looking her best. Her shimmering shoulder-length blond hair was in sharp contrast to the navy woolen suit with a white silk collar. She threw a navy-and-white scarf around her neck. The sun shone brilliantly, adding warmth to the weather, which hovered in the low sixties.

"Marble Arch, please," Fiona said.

"Yes, madam," the Indian taxi driver replied.

It was a slow process as Fiona gazed out the dust-laden window. The possibility of seeing Lord Von Pragh caused Fiona's heart to skip a beat. She bided her time and saw an older short-haired woman with a straw hat and orange square tinted glasses framing an oval-shaped face. Looming in front of Fiona was a grey stone wall, which had weathered decades of time and grime. It portrayed a youthful trampy-looking woman with dark-red nail polish. Her legs were crossed, revealing bony knees. A cigarette dangled from her right hand in an attempt to lure passersby to buy that brand of cigarettes.

A bicyclist passed near Fiona's side within collision distance with a red hook on the handlebar. On the sidewalk, a thirtyish dark-haired man walked along, somberly dressed in black with black knee-high boots. A heavy silver chain dangled from his pocket. The traffic was getting heavier, causing Fiona's conveyance to drive at a crawl. A driver was helping a woman with expensive luggage from a trunk.

Fiona hoped she would be on time. At this juncture, doubt assailed her. A motorist was resting his jaw on his hand while another hand held the wheel. Then there was the taxi driver with no hand on the wheel. Passengers were exiting taxis and counting out single pound notes with frowns. As the taxi moved further along, there were throngs of people of all ages lining the streets.

"I'm not going further, madam," the Indian said. "I'm likely to have my taxi battered by this mob. The police are gonna have their hands full."

"That's OK," Fiona replied.

"You be careful out there. Anything can happen. Not in all my days in London when I first came here from India have I seen tempers so heated."

"I didn't expect to see so many."

"When it comes to parting with money, everybody gets involved."

The rally had begun in earnest, with people joining the ranks wherever there was space. They had placards in their hands, some of them put together by not-so-artistic individuals.

The placard said, "Conservatives be damned."

Further along there was an effigy of Harold Macmillan. Someone threw gasoline and match to it.

"No more taxes," bellowed the match lighter, who was joined by a chorus of enraged people.

"Will the Conservatives feed us when we have no food on the table?" said another, his voice dripping with sarcasm.

"By God, no," a petulant frizzy-haired woman said.

The mob walked along, stomping their feet, Fiona included. There was a blind man with a white cane and seeing brown Labrador retriever, the latter nervous by all the commotion. A man with a prosthetic leg tried to keep pace with the others. People stood idly by till they joined forces, marching along, spewing their mouths off at the latest arrival of conservatively dressed people who joined the ranks enthusiastically.

Fiona walked along somberly, her eyes furtively searching for the group from church. They were nowhere in sight.

A wooden makeshift cross said, "God does not allow us to tax our children more than they can bear."

Another sign said, "May the wrath of God bear down heavily with a vengeance on the Conservatives."

A man bellowed into the bullhorn, "Out with Macmillan. In with Labor."

A skin head turned to the crowd and said, "Out with Macmillan. In with Labor."

The refrain was repeated down the lines. The voices started quietly at first. They were joined by others till the same slogan was repeated throughout the route. The police urged people to stay in line and not sway against the steel barricades. Fiona heard the menacing thud of a drum from some quarter. Men clenched their fists, threw them in the air, and chanted.

There was a dog walker with a sleek black-and-tan Doberman pincher, the latter barking viciously at the noisemaker. The dog walker shortened the leash, pulling the dog closer to him. Shop signs had their say too, with notices condemning the proposed new tax law. The rallying crowd halted.

Curious, Fiona stood on tiptoe. Her breath came in a short gasp. Standing in the midst of the demonstrators was Lord Von Pragh. Immediately she felt like dashing to him to ensure his safety and was in no harm's way with the enraged crowd. All too clearly, she realized that with the surge of the crowd, he could be trampled. If that happened, there would be no way she could fend her way through the masses to be near this magnificent hunk of a blind man.

"Robert!" Fiona cried out.

He seemed oblivious to her and genuinely interested in being part of the mob. Honking cars grew louder as police tried to still the instigator. Others honked furiously, creating a din. Taxis were bumper to bumper as weary and agitated passengers exited in disgust. The traffic lights changed to green, and still the cars moved at a snail's pace. Flat and store windows were thrown up. Office workers and housewives egged on the demonstrators.

Fiona was shoved as she again called out to Robert while waving her hand. The noise was deafening, between the honking of horns and the chorus of voices joining in. There seemed to be a glimmer of recognition, because Robert turned to Fiona. But she didn't stand a hair's breadth of a chance of getting near him.

Robert moved gingerly with his cane to the edge of the sidewalk and said, "Fiona."

A young lady stepped aside and urged her corpulent male companion to do likewise. Fiona reached out her hand. What a thrill it was to feel the hot blood on a cold day pulsing through his veins as he cupped her hand protectively, if not possessively.

Loud enough so that he could be heard above the din, he said, "How I missed you." He plonked a hard, wet kiss on her lips.

Caught unaware and by surprise, Fiona did not have time to respond in the way she would have liked. Giddy with ecstasy, she was silent and knew by the throb in his voice that he meant what he said. Inwardly she was delighted and tried to hide that fact. Did her eyes betray her? she wondered. At times she forgot he was blind. It was so good to hear his deep, melodious voice again. She put her hands through his. Now she felt so confident. Lurking in her mind were promptings that this man must be punished for the shocking treatment of women in the past. While it was pointless trying to talk to him because of the pushing and shoving from all angles, she had to admit that she was the luckiest woman to be in the company of Lord Von Pragh. She felt at one with him, something she had never felt before.

To herself, Fiona acknowledged that no human being should be trodden on, and certainly not to the point of desperation culminating in suicide. She noticed the shock on Lord Von Pragh's face when she made no response. Perhaps he was wondering if she was dickering with his feelings.

Truthfully, Fiona was torn between admitting her love for Lord Von Pragh, while at the same time proving to him that she would not be taken for granted. Although it was perplexing to her, she realized it must be bothering him a great deal. But he was master of the game—older, wiser, and more experienced. She doubted that she would emerge from this unscathed.

Although Fiona's many activities kept her busy, always the figure of Lord Von Pragh loomed before her. Why was she interested in what he was doing? Was it jealousy rearing its ugly head, or a natural concern for him because of his psychic blindness?

Clinging tenaciously to him lest she lose him, was this compulsion to take care of Lord Von Pragh? Placards wafted in the afternoon breezes. Voices drowned out her thoughts. The crowd scattered in all directions, indicating that the demonstration was over.

Reluctantly Fiona said, "I have to go now."

"Without me?" he asked, a quizzical look on his face.

"You could come to our healing session."

"That's not for me much as I want to be with you."

As he had experienced so often in the past, that cold sensation engulfed Fiona. Was that the presence of his meddlesome dead wife again? Must she continue to torment Fiona? Was it she who had prompted Lord Von Pragh to refuse outright her request to attend the healing session?

Was his dead wife punishing Lord Von Pragh for something he had done in the past or perhaps failed to do? Fiona saw the glimmer of recognition on Robert's face. It was all too clear that Fiona was to be the third party in everything that transpired between them.

Yet Fiona wondered why she should resent the never-ending presence of Robert's deceased wife. In fact, she was not an unwelcome entity. She had interfered at every twist and turn in their relationship. She had served her purpose. On whom was she seeking revenge? Fiona or Lord Von Pragh?

Was Fiona becoming selfish and bitter? She tried to banish the notion that she was jealous of Robert's dead wife. As much as she trusted her London lawyer, he would have no time for the ramblings of Fiona. The story of a presence she could describe would be too preposterous for the likes of a hard-nosed man of logic her father had chosen to manage his will.

Was it the influence of the full moon that made Fiona so indecisive and muddled? There seemed to be a restlessness in the air and a danger lurking somewhere. There was no other accounting for it other than the full moon.

Citizens were angry and vented their rage in the streets and alleys of London. There was a sense of urgency and change hovering around Fiona. She had no recourse but to go with the flow. She knew not where it would take her. It had to be a situation better than her current predicament.

Lord Von Pragh said, "I want to be alone with you, Fiona."

Arm in arm they strolled leisurely along the cobbled streets. Fiona could hardly believe her luck that she was with the most prized man of London. Vanished were her hopeless thoughts of last week and the accompanying despondence. Fiona's heart was light, as if a huge burden had been lifted from her shoulders. She heard footsteps behind her. Although a distinct feeling of unease seized her, Fiona was reluctant to look behind. This was civilized London. Besides, she had her most powerful ally at her side. Was there anything else she could wish? She clutched his arm more fiercely.

Suddenly a brawny, weather-beaten red-skinned man with a satanic gleam in his eyes jumped ahead of Lord Von Pragh. His brittle red hair was standing on end. Was he going to stop them dead in their tracks? Fiona and Lord Von Pragh halted.

"'Tis you I'm looking for, milord," the stranger said, and his fist was clenched in a raised position.

"What is the nature of your business?" Lord Von Pragh said without flickering a muscle in his face.

"I've 'ad a beef against you since that beautiful cousin of mine was killed by you. Yeah! She died of a broken 'eart."

"She killed herself. For that I am sorry."

"She was good enough to use and for you to go to bed with. Not good enough to marry the likes of you. Eh?"

Without provocation, he punched Lord Von Pragh in the face. Lord Von Pragh stiffened.

"What is it you want from me?"

"I want nothing. You see, there are people in life who aren't begging at the feet of the rich."

The man's face became redder and his voice more threatening as he spoke. His huge rough hands with dirty nails grabbed Lord Von Pragh's throat. The latter reached up to remove his hands.

"I'm gonna kill you," the stranger said, "as you killed my gentle cousin."

Fiona wanted to step between them. She realized it could be very dangerous. The stranger tightened his grip on Lord Von Pragh. Fiona looked around helplessly. She watched her boyfriend's eyes bulge. His arms rose and fingers splayed and stiffened. His cane dropped to the ground.

Without further ado, Fiona reached down and grabbed the cane. She straightened up. With a merciless blow, she hit the attacker on the head once and then twice. The attacker released his grip and slumped to the stone sidewalk.

"Are you all right, Robert?" she enquired, adjusting his necktie.

She caressed her hand gently across his face. Without thinking, she kissed him on the cheek. He looked at her seriously and said, "You saved my life, Fiona."

"I had to do something." There was reproach in her voice.

She glanced around furtively to see if anybody had witnessed what had transpired.

Lord Von Pragh said, "If you hadn't done that, I'd be dead."

"God forbid."

"Do I mean that much to you?"

Without hesitation, she said, "Yes. More than you know."

For one brief moment, she thought she had killed the stranger. They both watched warily as he was moving his feet. What if he had sustained a fractured skull or bleeding in the brain? There were no witnesses to corroborate the event.

Fiona reached out her hand to the stunned man.

"What the bloody . . . 'ell 'appened. Where am I?"

"Someone struck you from behind."

"I don't remember that."

"Really?"

"I thought . . . a bobby . . . had hit me with a nightstick. It wouldn't be the first time."

Even though Fiona felt like bursting out laughing, a quiver of panic gripped her stomach. She bent down and asked the dazed man if she could examine his head. Fortunately for her, there was no evidence of blood when he parted his hair to pinpoint the site of the pain. A lump the size of a half crown, reddish blue in color, had formed on the scalp.

"Am I all right?" he enquired sheepishly.

"The skin isn't broken."

"I'm as thick as a plank."

"It doesn't seem too bad."

"Ooh! Now me 'ead is beginning to hurt."

"Of course, and it will for a few days, I'd imagine. Let me help you."

"No." There was indication that he would brook no interference.

He bent his knees, and with palms on the ground, he got up very slowly. He staggered. Lord Von Pragh wisely moved aside.

"Who the 'ell are you?" the attacker snapped.

"Somebody you don't want to know," Lord Von Pragh replied.

"You're right. Me bloody 'ead is killing me."

"If the pain gets really bad," Fiona said, "you should go to the doctor."

"Not a bad idea, pretty face," he said with a mischievous grin. "Thanks for yer help."

"Get home before dark," she said, hoping that nothing worse should befall him in transit.

What if the police found him dead? What if he lapsed into a coma and wound up in the hospital? There would be an investigation. Surely one of his relatives had known of his intention. Fiona would be branded a murderer. She glanced around and up to the buildings to see if anyone had seen her striking the man. There was always the possibility of some tenant lurking in the window or a nosey individual who had nothing better to do.

It was now Fiona's business to see if someone had seen her raise the cane and deliver a deadly blow that would have killed a man half the size of the aggressor. Why hadn't she the good sense and forethought to hit him on the back or on his broad muscular shoulders?

As Fiona watched the man stumble away, she breathed a sigh of relief and said, "Thank the Lord he's a big man."

"I'll have to hide my cane from you," Lord Von Pragh said, "if ever you get annoyed with me." There was a sparkle of tenderness in his eyes.

"What was I to do? Let him choke you to death?"

"I didn't think you cared so much for me."

"I do."

"Show me more often. A man likes outward displays of affection and love. For the last couple of years, I've known scorn and contempt."

"I know it's been hard on you. But the despair of a woman in love bothers me."

Falling in love was a game of chance. Secretly she believed that she loved him more than he liked her. How was she to know? A dilemma it was meant to be. Or was it? How Fiona wished that she could throw her arms around Lord Von Pragh's neck and tell him unabashedly how he meant so much to her. Why did she have to hide her feelings? Perhaps he was too afraid of rejection.

"Whatever you may say about Christiana," Lord Von Pragh said, "I think she's my guardian spirit."

"Why do you say that?"

"I communicate with her clairaudiently, and many a time I receive advice."

"Of course, I believe in that."

"Remember how I told you in Bedford Castle that my senses have been heightened since this blindness set in? I don't want you to breathe a word about this to anyone. They'll think I'm a weirdo. It's a secret between just the two of us. As a member of Parliament, they would boot me out of office. I am clairvoyant, clairaudient, and clairsentient, meaning I see, I hear, and I feel."

"I won't say a word because I know of too many skeptics. I believe wholeheartedly in these psychic phenomena."

"For one thing, the enormous risk of investing a lot of my money with the American artist was a huge undertaking. It was also an extremely slow starter. Now the BBC cannot get enough material to keep the show in business. They're even thinking of putting it on at primetime, so popular is the show with children and even adults."

To herself, Fiona was thinking that she must inform her lawyer as soon as possible so that the stigma of Lord Von Pragh being a fortune hunter could be banished once and for all time.

"I'm delighted to hear that," Fiona said after a lengthy pause.

"I thought you would. Nothing ventured, nothing gained has always been my philosophy."

"That attitude surprises me."

"Why should it? When I met you in Bedford Castle, I imagined you to be the last person to take a risk"

"Risks in love are quite a different matter to business risks. I'm learning to be cautious in affairs of the heart."

"I didn't think other people's feelings were a high priority with you."

"You're the last lady I want to hurt, Fiona, even though you doubt me. I hope through time and circumstance I've changed."

"So do I."

"I'd never deliberately hurt you."

He looked her directly in the eyes with a fierceness mixed with gentleness, which was unnerving.

"Yes." There was irritation in his voice.

Without saying a word, Fiona felt that she was certainly justifiable to question the integrity of his intentions. Other people had to with good reason. They were trying to protect Fiona from a man whom they regarded as a monster in love, a satyr, a hedonist whose past had caught up with him.

If Lord Von Pragh were such a callous individual, Fiona reasoned, why then did no woman try to latch on to him even in death? Surely he must have treated Christiana with the utmost kindness and consideration. The idea of protecting Fiona's feelings was a significant sign that his laissez-faire attitude towards women had disappeared. At least one matter was laid to rest. Lord Von Pragh was not a fortune hunter, although never had Fiona considered him to be such.

It was with an exultant feeling that Fiona went to bed that night. Her fears of what others had said, including scurrilous newspaper accounts that he had described in great detail, were vanquished. Not that she had entertained them too seriously from the beginning. Newspapers' function was to tell citizens the goings-on in the world.

Yet a semblance of fear lurked in Fiona. She believed the stories about Lord Von Pragh's womanizing. But maybe time and harrowing experience had forced him to change his ways. Or had they?

But Fiona must not condemn her lawyer. As he had said, Fiona's interests were of the utmost importance, hence his revelation that Lord Von Pragh was a person of dubious character.

Thank goodness Fiona had trusted her instinct. She had implicitly believed in Lord Von Pragh from the time she had seen him weeping inconsolably in Bedford Castle.

Back in her flat, it suddenly dawned on Fiona that an anger such as she had not experienced before arose in her at the sight of a stranger assaulting Lord Von Pragh. No matter how well intentioned the stranger's cause, Fiona was not about to tolerate it. Wasn't that only a natural reaction? However, she realized that it wasn't she who had whammed the aggressor on the head. It was another force.

It reminded her that the unearthly force was none other than Lord Von Pragh's deceased wife. It was as if Christiana had snatched the cane from the ground and dealt a ferocious blow to the man's head, a blow so violent that it could have rendered the attacker unconscious. Thinking about it realistically, it could have been a mortal blow with deadly consequences for Fiona too.

For that reason, Fiona considered Christiana in a more serious light. Was she evil? Was she capable of grievously hurting another? Was her intention to protect Lord Von Pragh, or get Fiona into trouble that could result in serving life in prison? By doing so she would separate Fiona and Lord Von Pragh. The more Fiona questioned it, the more rational thinking eluded her.

By no means was it in Fiona's pattern of behavior to be cruel and oblivious to the plight of another human being. Did this stranger have justification for repaying for his cousin's death? Fiona wished she knew more.

On the other hand, Fiona owed a debt of gratitude to Lord Von Pragh. He was not a murderer, but a man who had an unstable mistress who killed herself. Lest she be judged for hurting a man, it was not for Fiona to judge. Why was Christiana Von Pragh so intent in getting Fiona into trouble with the law? Why was she not at rest like most dead spirits? Was it her all-consuming mission that hovered at every twist and turn? Was it the presence of Fiona at his side that enraged her? Was it because of Lord Von Pragh's psychic blindness that Christiana wanted to be near him, to protect and nurture? Had love eluded her prior to meeting Lord Von Pragh?

Was Christiana walking by his side because she had not yet found contentment amongst other spirits?

The answer was elusive, to say the least. Was Christiana holding Lord Von Pragh's hand lest he should stumble and fall? Fiona did not like the idea of being Christiana's instrument. It was disconcerting. Yet Fiona thought that Christiana must rest. Spirit people needed to rest at one time or another. Christiana's intentions may be good, but her actions indicated that she would use any means at her disposal to ensure that Lord Von Pragh would be alone with her.

Fiona knew that it was possible to communicate with spirit friends and loved ones. Now her only wish was that Lord Von Pragh's deceased wife would move into the nonearthly realm, where she belonged.

So surprised was Lord Von Pragh when Fiona went to his penthouse in the mews to discuss the next forthcoming rally that he swept her into his arms. He tilted her chin up and pressed hard on her mouth. At first she was resistant and shy.

Fiona decided to throw caution to the wind. Her lips were lush and lavish as she savored his kisses. His tongue was deep and probing, causing Fiona to feel weak and then intoxicated with delight. She felt a tingling sensation down her body. Her nipples were taut, responding to his gentle maneuvers. He kissed her stomach, causing waves of rapture to her legs and permeating all over. She wanted him to experience the same warm glow, the awakening to a new sensation.

Yet in some way, Fiona felt inadequate. How was she to compare to the many former lovers of Lord Von Pragh and especially to his wife? He took her hand in his and led her to the bed with its fringed canopy.

Fiona was all restraint. Lord Von Pragh opened a bottle of bubbly Perrier-Jouët champagne. He drank his slowly while Fiona sipped hers. Not used to imbibing, she felt giddy. Was it the anticipation of lovemaking or the champagne? It mattered not. It was a good feeling. Slowly he undressed her, relishing the contours of her body. She glanced towards his eyes and thought she detected a spiritual quality about them. Then they seemed to transform, making Fiona feel uncertain. Was it madness she detected, or was it passion? How would she be able to differentiate?

Scrolling her body, Lord Von Pragh unzipped Fiona's skirt and let it drop to the plush carpet. Unbuttoning her blouse, it was out of the question for her to resist. He led her closer to the white quilted bed. A fragrant scent of cedar hit her nostrils. Like a woman in a trance, she responded to his kisses, which at times were gentle alternating with a ferocity.

Never before had Fiona felt so alive and vibrating with raw emotion that could not be quenched. Gone was the unthinkable fact that his wife might intervene. Fiona pressed Lord Von Pragh possessively to her. Her legs quivered with the intensity of hot pulsing fever. Fiona was lost, lost in another world that she wished she could inhabit forever, locked in Lord Von Pragh's embrace. Such shivers of delight flooded through her body. This was a man who aroused in her nonearthly sensations. What trick was this? she wondered.

Now Fiona was certain that she had ignited something that had lain dormant. Gone was Lord Von Pragh's brooding and self-loathing, and in its place were his hands and lips tracing down her naked neck. She wanted to push him away gently, but she would not and, if she were honest, could not. This was a man of gentle fierceness who roamed his tongue all over her braless breasts.

A boldness that was foreign to Fiona's nature reared its head. She wanted to arouse Lord Von Pragh to the point of no return. An aching, longing sensation jolted her into submission. He kissed the soft mound of blonde pubic hair. She hurtled higher and higher like a volcano that had defied the gods. She wanted to take him, to possess him. She would brook no interference. His tongue slid lower, twirling her with pleasure. She let out several soft moans.

From the corner of her eye, Fiona saw the soft white billowy window curtain. In her exalted state, she thought she imagined it. Was it ecstasy that caused a cold sensation? Nonsense, she concluded. Not for one minute did she wish to be jolted back to reality.

On his knees, Lord Von Pragh was about to penetrate her. "Fuck my brains out, Fiona," he said.

She admired the muscular strength and agility of his body. A rising tide of resentment stemmed within her. From behind the curtain, a white ghostly form appeared. It seemed to be moving ever closer towards Fiona. That cold sensation was present. There was no mistake about it. It wasn't her imagination. Was that form moving again?

Suddenly Lord Von Pragh plopped to the bed. Fiona reached out and took a sip of the now flat champagne. She nestled him closer as he lay writhing by her side. His face was dark and stormy as she tried to quench the quivering of her body. She felt pampered and protected when he drew her closer to him. He placed his hand tenderly between her legs, dulling the quivering within.

"I'm sorry," he said.

"Don't worry. It was so wonderful I wanted it to last all day and all night."

"So did I," he said, his voice a whisper.

Too well did Fiona know that it would be unwise to bring up the interference of his wife. She knew that Christiana Von Pragh had intervened when she suspected that there would be no turning back.

Fiona nestled closer to Lord Von Pragh, stroking his long lean muscular body. He took her hand and entwined her fingers within his. Instinctively Fiona felt they belonged to each other. Or was it merely a figment of her imagination? How could he belong to her when a dead wife beckoned him elsewhere? Fiona was simply deluding herself. But she cared not one iota whether it was a delusion.

Fiona must have Lord Von Pragh to herself. He must belong to her, not as a piece of goods or chattel to be owned. She wanted him, to love and protect him. Was it asking too much? she questioned. Why couldn't she have been lucky to meet a normal man without strings attached? It was either Fiona's fortune or misfortune. Only time would tell.

The truth was that Fiona could not reveal that she was in love—hook, line, and sinker—with Lord Von Pragh. How else could she explain the quiet contentment she felt entwined in his arms as if united by destiny? She must relish these moments, lest they should not come this way again.

Was this how Christiana felt with Lord Von Pragh? Was it any wonder that Fiona could not part with him? Suddenly she felt afraid. Wasn't this the reason that his mistress committed suicide? When she couldn't have him in marriage, she died by her own hand. Fiona believed that her pain must have been excruciating. She hoped that the same fate should not befall her. They lay quietly, not uttering a word. Fiona's mind raced with possibilities of being hurt by Lord Von Pragh. Why should she be an exception? If she was foolish enough to fall in love with him, she must suffer the consequences. For now Fiona was in a blissful state. Let it last, she implored.

CHAPTER 17

"Hello!" Fiona said when she answered the ringing phone. Secretly she hoped it would be Lord Von Pragh. It was quite early in the morning, with sparrows singing and pigeons cooing.

"Is this Fiona Morgan?" the male voice enquired.

"Yes. This is she."

"This is the music director of the Royal Opera House at Covent Garden. I have a golden opportunity for you to sing at our opera house on the eastern fringes of the West End as soon as possible."

Fiona was speechless for several minutes before she gasped, "Why? What happened?"

"Our star soloist fractured her hip in an accident, leaving us totally unprepared for the unknown. Apparently, it is a serious break, and I don't expect her back for a long time. Her stand-in is on holiday in Las Palmas in the Canary Islands. I don't know when she'll be back either."

"I can't believe this. I'll be there at noon."

Hurrying to look her best, Fiona brushed her hair and threw on a smart olive-green dress. She was whisked in a limousine to the venerable awe-inspiring Royal Opera House of Edwardian architectural style. Music with accompanying instruments emanated from the stage.

The music director said, "I know you've been practicing your singing every day."

"I'm very nervous," she said in a hushed tone.

"That's only natural. But your voice coach tells me you're making terrific strides."

"That is encouraging."

Fiona was introduced to the orchestral musicians including the conductor, pianist, flutist, harpist, saxophonist, drummer, and others.

"We'll dispense with the makeup and costume now," the music director said.

"However, tomorrow evening, you'll have to be here four hours in advance. You have quite a singer to match."

With all the pathos she could command, Fiona glued her eyes to the conductor and his baton. Scheduled to sing the role of Mimi of *La Bohème*, she proceeded with the singing. She was extremely tired at the end of the session. Hardy able to believe her good luck, Fiona was driven home in a tired, exalted state of mind. Nevertheless, doubt assailed her.

Was Fiona's singing up to the standard of the Royal Opera House? After all, people flocked to this place from all over the world. Who was the singer she was replacing? What if the patrons didn't like her? After all, attendees paid good money to see and hear their favorite opera star. Fiona was an unknown except in church. She wanted to proclaim to the world about her good fortune and especially to Lord Von Pragh. Trying to contact him via phone was to no avail. Fiona wondered why the news of the opera star's accident was not in the news. That night she was hardly able to eat or sleep; so excited was she. After tossing and turning for an hour, she decided to meditate. Eventually she drifted off to sleep.

Exhilarated, Fiona went to Covent Garden the next day. There was precious little time to notice the fruit sellers, the flower sellers, the fishmongers, and assorted people doing one thing or another. Arriving at the Royal Opera House, she headed to the costume room. The seamstress fitted her with a black drab dress, which needed some adjustment. From there she went to the makeup artist. A humming humidifier kept her vocal chords moist.

White pancake foundation and a touch of blush were applied to both cheeks. A bluish-tinge lipstick outlined her full lips. Black eyeliner made her eyes sunken looking followed by black mascara. When she examined herself in the mirror at the finished look, Fiona thought she looked ghastly.

"I look awful," Fiona confided.

"That's how you're supposed to be in the role of the dying Mimi. Her body was ravaged by tuberculosis."

It seemed no length of time before Fiona's premier performance. However, she waited in the wings while the music director made a special announcement.

"Good evening, ladies and gentlemen. I am sorry to be the bearer of bad tidings. Our favorite opera star had an unforeseen accident. We all send her our best wishes for a speedy recovery. Fiona Morgan will replace her tonight. Let's give her a warm welcome."

"Oh no!" was the exclamation from many quarters of the opera house.

Peeping out through the heavy red velvet curtain fringed with gold embroidery, Fiona observed people get up and leave. Gosh! Would there be enough patrons left to hear her? she thought. Feeling downhearted, Fiona resolved to show them that she could be as good as the injured opera star. Quietly she said a prayer to her grandmother and, with faltering footsteps, moved to the center of the stage with a newfound confidence. The reception was lukewarm, to say the least.

From the depths of her heart and taking note of her breathing, Fiona sang the role of Mimi with a resignation to her suffering. After the first scene, when the curtain closed on her, Fiona believed that the applause was mediocre. How could an unknown like her compete with the former reigning diva? She would have to dig into the depths of her soul and emote feeling.

After the intermezzo, Fiona glanced out at the audience. She thought she detected Lord Von Pragh. How could she be sure it was him? Her heart leapt with delight, and she vowed to make him proud of her. After all, music was in his soul. Of course, it was quite possible that he was a member of the audience. If Fiona had nothing else in common with him, at least music united them. In many ways, she knew he was a blind kindred spirit. Maybe because of his psychic agnosia he felt more deeply than most souls.

LOVE THAT NEVER DIES

At the completion of scene 2, the audience seemed to be more receptive to Fiona. Nobody walked out, for which she was grateful, even though there were quite a few empty seats in the house. Yes. That was Lord Von Pragh without a doubt, applauding tumultuously with vacant seats on either side of him. Fiona bowed her head and smiled triumphantly towards him. He would be able to compare her to the injured opera star. Or was he just being kind and appreciative? The lights dimmed, and there was a short intermission.

By the time of the final scene, Fiona put her heart and soul into the dying Mimi's farewell, remembering her coach's admonition. As if emanating from the grave, her voice was weak and thready. Before the completion, she heard applause from the audience. They were tumultuous and in awe of her performance, many sniffling and wiping their eyes. Closing her eyes so that she could savor the applause, the curtain closed on her, separating her from Lord Von Pragh. "Encore! Encore!" patrons shouted.

The curtain reopened. An elderly tuxedoed man threw a garland of roses onto the stage, almost hitting Fiona. Feeling overwhelmed, she suppressed a tear brimming in her eye. Then Lord Von Pragh stood up, followed slowly by others. Within minutes the audience was on their feet.

In acknowledgement, she bowed gracefully to the center and the side aisles, prolonging her bow where Lord Von Pragh stood alone. Mesmerize her he did, although she did not want to admit it. Reporters, critics, photographers, and television newsmen rushed backstage when Fiona entered the dressing room.

"Who are you?" they wanted to know. Fiona was unable to handle the numerous questions coming from so many experts.

The music director said, "One question at a time, please."

"But we want to know all about the reigning opera star," a television newsman said impatiently.

"Is this wondrous voice in the genes?" a well-known critic enquired.

"My father was not in the arts. He was a businessman," Fiona said.

"Who was your mother?" a reporter asked.

"Somebody I never met," Fiona said with downcast eyes.

Before he could say another word, Lord Von Pragh with his cane entered into the hullabaloo.

"No more questions, please," he said. "Can't you see that Ms. Morgan is exhausted?" His voice was adamant.

"But the world wants to know everything about this beautiful, talented singer," the critic snapped.

The photographer said, "I know you from somewhere. I never forget a face. It's my business. That's my bread and butter. I remember the cane. Let me think about this. It'll come to me soon." Pressing his hand to his temple, the photographer said, "Yes. Now I got it. You were the young lady who bashed the fellow on the head, knocking him out cold with Lord Von Pragh's cane. I thought the poor bugger was dead, but apparently he is not. The police are searching for you."

Unable to deny it, Fiona wanted to run from the dressing room. Instead she said, "He was trying to choke Lord Von Pragh. He is a blind man. I had to intervene."

"You're one tough lady," the photographer said with a touch of cynicism in his voice. "I'm not surprised that you wound up here at the prestigious Royal Opera House."

"It was Ms. Morgan's hard work and patience," said Lord Von Pragh, "that resulted in tonight's performance."

"To whom do you owe your extraordinary talent?" the acerbic critic enquired.

"My church singing, which refined and polished my voice."

"No more questions," the music director said. "Let's celebrate with champagne for Ms. Morgan and all of you."

Rolled in on a cart were several decanters of champagne and crystal flutes.

"Don't drink too much, Fiona," Lord Von Pragh cautioned. "You may blabber something that's nobody's business."

"I'll be very discreet," she answered.

But the critic was insistent and said, "Fiona, why would you hit someone and knock him out cold, resulting in bleeding in the brain?"

"I never meant to do that. Honestly."

"You realize, do you not, that the police probably have an all-out bulletin searching for you?"

Fiona wanted to burst out crying. She did not know whether they were searching for her due to the mayor of Limerick's son, Rory McCormack, or because of her propensity to violence as the critic had said.

While Lord Von Pragh was talking to the newsmen, the photographer approached her and whispered into her ear. He handed her a note with his business card.

Rushing to the bathroom, she opened the note. "Meet me tomorrow at the Jacqueranda Club at one o'clock."

Returning to the dressing room, Fiona felt confused. Should she tell Lord Von Pragh? What kind of business would she discuss with the photographer? Was he interested in her? Certainly she had eyes for no one but Lord Von Pragh. Did the photographer want to make a contract with her or glorify his own name? Uncertainty lurked in her so that she was hardly able to notice the cameras flashing pictures of her.

Toasting Fiona, Lord Von Pragh said, "Let's go home."

The director of the Royal Opera House said, "Not yet. We have to introduce Ms. Morgan to the many attendees eager to see her. We can never let down our public."

"I forgot about that," Lord Von Pragh said sheepishly.

There was pushing and shoving at the back exit so that Fiona thought they would break the steel door down.

Loud voices said, "We want Ms. Morgan. We want Ms. Morgan."

Taking Lord Von Pragh's hand, Fiona said, "Please come with me."

"No. This is your night to shine." He pressed her hand reassuringly.

"Open the door," a loud male voice said, knocking on the door. "I can't control this crowd any longer."

The narrow steel door opened. The mob pushed and surged forward.

The photographer barked, "Let me through."

"Good," said someone. "Take our picture."
"I'm here to take Ms. Morgan's photo."
"What about us?" another person said.
"Step aside, please," the burly security said.

Fiona glanced behind her to see Lord Von Pragh. However, the door was closed.

"Congratulations, Ms. Morgan!" several well-wishers said.
"A new star is born," a well-dressed Englishman said.

Even though she was extremely tired, Fiona signed autographs for several people. It was better, she believed, than talking as her voice needed a rest. George Gronback recorded her every movement on camera. She shook hands with many in the crowd, some squeezing so tightly that it hurt. Others had limp handshakes. There were those with sweaty palms and other frail people with cold hands. However, Fiona knew that this was the evening she had hoped and waited for. The music director looked on in appreciation.

Lurking in the back of her mind was Lord Von Pragh. What was he doing? Sipping champagne while Fiona relished in the glory? This must not be, she thought. She wanted him at her side to reveal her true feelings, that he was more important than her career. He must not be ignored. Would she relinquish her career for him? Absolutely, in a minute, although it was her lifetime aspiration. Her dream had come true, but would it bring true happiness? If he abandoned her for another woman, she did not believe she could go on. Or could she? Maybe she would devote her life to opera singing.

The security guard stepped towards Fiona and whispered, "Lord Von Pragh wants to go home now."

"OK. Let's go inside."

"Good night, Ms. Morgan," cried the well-wishers.

She threw them kisses till Lord Von Pragh pulled her to him in the doorway. When the door closed, he kissed her deeply and passionately, enveloping her in a cocoon of love and safety. Oblivious to how long it lasted, she wanted it to go on forever.

"Come on, you lovebirds," the director said. "The limousine is waiting."

Fiona sat in the backseat with Lord Von Pragh. The music director sat opposite them. Holding her hand, Lord Von Pragh closed his eyes. Within a few minutes, he was snoring. The music director switched seats to be near Fiona.

He whispered, "That magnificent perfume you're wearing turns me on."

He trailed his hand down her thigh till he reached above her knee. He pulled up her dress and slithered his hand between her legs.

"Kiss me," he said, his voice hushed and demanding.

"No," she said, pulling his hand away.

"He can't see anything. What are you worried about?"

Attempting to meet her mouth, Fiona pressed the tips of her fingers against Lord Von Pragh's hands. The music director insisted again that Fiona give him a kiss. She pushed him away with such force that she hardly knew she was capable of such an act. He glared at her angrily.

Wiping sweat from his brow, he said, "Is that all the thanks I get for making you a star?"

"I'm sorry. I didn't think it entailed this type of stuff."

"I saw how you kissed that blind man. Why can't I enjoy the same treatment?"

"Work is work and pleasure is pleasure, and the twain never shall meet."

Lord Von Pragh stirred and said, "I was in a semitrance. Keep your hands off, old boy, or there'll be fireworks. Would your wife like to hear about this behavior? I'm blind, but that doesn't mean I'm deaf and dumb."

"Sorry, Lord Von Pragh. I thought we are all out for fun."

"Let me tell you. She's my darling. I love her and will not tolerate anyone disrespecting her."

The music director proffered his hand to Lord Von Pragh. They shook hands, but it was obvious that Lord Von Pragh did not regard it lightly. At the railway station, the music director stepped out of the limousine with a scowl.

"I'm glad you woke up," Fiona said. I don't know what he was up to."

"Remember this, Fiona. Men are animals with too much testosterone flooding their bodies."

"I want you to be an animal with me."

"Not tonight. I'm tired, but very soon I'll make it up to you."

"I can't wait. I want to bring out the beast in you."

Next day with the rain glistening on the cobbled pavement under flashes of lightning and thunder rolling in the heavens, Fiona thought it would be a temporary storm. She shook her umbrella, which had turned inside out several times on the way to the Jacqueranda Club. This was going to be a miraculous day, she hoped. The entrance to the place was a stone courtyard leading to a very dimly lit club. Small white candles flickered in red glass containers. Jazz music played softly in the background. Three large Afghan dogs rested peacefully by a handsome woman's chair.

Fiona recognized George and beckoned him to join her at the banquette. He sat beside Fiona.

"Is this your treat or mine?" he enquired.

"Absolutely mine."

"I'm sure," he said, "you're wondering why I asked you to meet me here."

"No doubt your intentions are honorable."

"I admire you very much."

"Thank you."

"Let's order first so that we have no interference. You never know who is listening. The waiters hear more than you know."

"You're right."

"What would you like?"

A tall, thin man with a pleasing Jamaican accent stood with a dupe pad. George ordered a pot of Earl Grey tea and sconces while for himself he ordered a vodka martini.

Returning hastily, the waiter said, "Will that be all?"

"For now, yes. Thank you," George said.

George glanced around furtively. Everyone seemed to be involved in the jazz music, which was soothing and comforting to Fiona's ears. He snuggled closer to Fiona.

"I like you," George said. "That's why I want to help you."

"That's very nice of you. But how can you help me?"

"As I said last night, we have a secret in common. Just the two of us. Nobody must know about this meeting, especially Lord Von Pragh."

"I can keep my business to myself."

"Can you? You know," he continued, "you could be in serious trouble with the law and facing a felony charge, which mandates a minimum of five years in jail."

"Don't remind me."

Immediately Fiona recalled Lord Von Pragh with his hands in a spatial position and thinking he would be gone forever more. Up to now, she had no regrets about saving him. However, she regarded it as a law of karma that she should pay for her misdeed.

"You're quiet," George said. "I have to get it into your head that I'm the only person who witnessed you strike the blow to that poor bugger's head. Believe me, only I can save you by keeping my mouth shut."

"You won't tell anyone. Will you?" There was an imploring tone to her voice.

"Omerta comes at a price. You can understand that."

"What's omerta?"

"The oath of silence. In some cultures, it comes under penalty of death. Thank goodness, they've abolished the death penalty here in England."

"You're scaring me."

George took a gulp of martini and said, "One hundred pounds will get you off the hook. It has to be cash. I don't take checks or credit cards." His eyes narrowed.

There was no mistaking the treachery behind them.

"Let me think about this," Fiona said after a long pause.

"What's to think about?"

"I know. I know . . . you're trying to . . . help me." Mulling it over in her head, Fiona tried to fathom whether she was doing the right thing. Something smelled fishy. But at this juncture in her career, she could not let anything stand in her way. If only Lord Von Pragh were at her side to guide her. This was a dicey situation.

"I'll tell you what, Fiona," George continued. "Do you want to pay me a mere one hundred pounds or pay some shark of a lawyer thousands of pounds to defend you at the Old Bailey courthouse? Even then, you won't know the outcome."

"God no."

"It's up to you. They'll drag your name and background through the mire. I'm sure there are certain matters that you don't want revealed. It's up to you."

Although Fiona knew that she could implicitly trust Lord Von Pragh, this serious matter she must only share with George, the photographer. While he waited in the Jacqueranda Club, she hastened to the bank. There she withdrew one hundred and forty pounds, enough to cover the hush money and the bill she owed. When she returned, the crowd was less. At the banquette she counted out under the table one hundred crisp notes in twenty denominations. He deposited one hundred pounds in his pants pocket. A small price, she figured, to cover her tracks. He left an unusually large tip, so what of it. His eyes met hers, and he thanked her.

"I'll leave first," he said.

"That's fine."

Fiona finished her sconces and pot of tea. Her mind wandering all over the place, she wondered whether George had photographs of her committing the act. She could not remember seeing the flash of a camera. Maybe he did it from a distance without her knowing it. Hoping that he did not have evidence to implicate her, she went home from the dingy nightclub. At least, this matter was settled once and for all. Or was it?

What if he knew the mayor of Limerick's son. It was quite possible. Was the photographer honest? she questioned. Rory McCormack certainly was not. Why did it take so long to realize that people are imperfect, particularly when it comes to money?

Lord Von Pragh was considered an odious character by many Londoners. Not in Fiona's eyes. He was the most noble and honorable man she had met. Yet how could she compare? For too long her life had been cloistered by the Ursuline nuns. This state of affairs was a rude awakening. She must face facts. There were a lot of unscrupulous people around, and she must protect herself from the snares surrounding her.

Between her hectic schedule of singing in church, the role of Mimi at the Royal Opera House, and attending the healing sessions, Fiona had little time to worry about Rory McCormack. Yet it lurked in her mind on a disturbingly frequent note. Why? Maybe he had forgotten her. At least, Lord Von Pragh was busy with the British broadcasting series. On an occasional evening, he came to the healing sessions. Although not a believer in Reiki healing, he claimed to be feeling much better at the conclusion.

At their last meeting, Lord Von Pragh had said, "Let's get away from London. My schedule is slow. Maybe we can be alone and enjoy each other."

"I'd love to do that. What place do you have in mind?"

"Somewhere relatively quiet. What do you say about St. Peter Port in the Channel Islands?"

"It sounds wonderful."

"My secretary will make the arrangements and let you know all the details where to meet me."

Fiona was exultant about being with Lord Von Pragh not surrounded by the noise and tumult of metropolitan living. While he loved living in London, she felt it would be in his interest to get away, not to mention for her sake too. After all, she was born in Ireland and favored the countryside. London was for getting ahead in life and fulfilling one's ambition. An island would be more easygoing and people less harried. She must go to a place where she was not known and not be bothered by crowds as happened at the Royal Opera House after her premiere performance. Here she would not be bombarded by fans as a celebrity. Native islanders would not have a clue about her ambition, her love life, and her wealth. She knew that the Channel Islands, which included Guernsey, Jersey, Alderney, and Sark, were haunts for English honeymooners.

"From there we can sail to France by hydrofoil. It's only a thirty-mile trip by boat to Marseilles," Lord Von Pragh said.

"Maybe the spirit that has dogged us will leave us alone."

"Spirit guides definitely serve a purpose."

"Oh! I'm really looking forward to our trip."

"There is one big problem. They won't let us share the same room in any hotel without the benefit of marriage or at least a wedding ring on my finger."

"That's easy to circumvent. I'll claim you're my nurse. After all, I'm disabled and suffer from psychic blindness. If it makes you more secure, I can get an official note from the top Harley Street specialist authenticating my agnosia."

"I'd feel more comfortable. I don't want to be embarrassed checking in at a hotel."

"You're with me. The deed is done."

"They could even call the police and who knows the ramifications of it. I wish I lived in Paris. I wouldn't have to go through this rigmarole."

"Well, we have to abide by English laws while we're on these shores."

Fiona was thrilled at the prospect of going on holiday with Lord Von Pragh. She wished she had gone with him to Ischia. The Channel Islands were known to be delightful islands. She knew that the Royal Air Force was still located there where they served as a refuge in World War II. She would be more than pleased to meet Lord Von Pragh's comrades. Her only hope was that they would like her. Maybe they preferred his deceased wife and would compare Fiona to Christiana. They would recount their old days of glory, and maybe Fiona would discover the magnetism that lured Lord Von Pragh to her even in death. Surely Fiona must mean something special to him if he wanted to share a holiday with her. They could visit the house where Charles Dickens wrote one of his major novels and see the channel where one of his daughters drowned.

Hardly able to wait in anticipation, Fiona started lining up her wardrobe that she was going to take with her. Performing at the Royal Opera House three nights a week kept her busy. She could barely wait for the scheduled date of departure. Summer was fading, with the weather getting cooler. However, she liked the temperate climate.

A brisk wind was blowing outside as Fiona packed her suitcase. The doorbell rang. She considered it a little strange due to the fact she had not let anyone in from the outside door.

"It's you, thank goodness, Fiona!" exclaimed her sister, Georgina.

"You caught me at an inopportune time."

"Sorry to intrude on you like this. We're here in London, my friend and I. We thought we could drop by. We came to see the Monique exhibition."

"I'll wait outside in one of the nearby places," the friend said.

Fiona felt she had no choice but to let her into her flat. There was no mention of her father, which perplexed Fiona.

"You like art then?" Fiona said.

"I adore it. I wish I could afford Picasso, Matisse, Van Gogh, and those wonderful artists who struggled so much in life, and in death they are revered with the paintings selling for a bundle."

"I'm afraid I'm ignorant about the latest up-and-coming artists."

"I'll sell you a painting if you like. It can only go up in value. Frankly, I need the money for an operation for my friend. You don't know, but doctors cost a fortune in the USA. My poor friend has cancer. The operation she needs can only be performed in Denmark. There is a good chance she can survive many, many years if the operation is successful."

All Fiona could concentrate on was the misery Lord Von Pragh had endured for the last two years. Nobody could help him. His life was at a standstill.

Georgina took a gulp of coffee and resumed, "I thought you'd be living high on the hog with all the money bequeathed by our father."

"That's not my style," Fiona said. "I'm involved in the more spiritual aspect of life. Money does not bring happiness. It can afford to give one a good life, but other than that, I see no advantage to lots of money. Some of the most tragic and miserable people in the world want for nothing but peace of mind."

"My friend wasn't born lucky like us. Maybe she is lucky because she is good-looking like you. She was abandoned at birth, grew up in foster homes where she was ill treated, and eventually when she was six years old, stashed away in an orphanage where she literally starved. You saw how thin she is."

"Yes. She did seem ill nourished. Of course, the cancer doesn't help."

"Won't you, please, Fiona, find it in your heart to help her? I'll repay all the money to you when I get my father's portion of the will." She burst out crying.

"Hush! You must not get so upset." Fiona put a comforting hand on her shoulder.

"You will help?" There was an imploring quality to her voice as she looked up under heavy mascaraed eyelashes.

"I'll see what I can do. I have to remind you that because of my age, I have no control over my money."

"What do you mean?" There was exasperation in her tone.

"The lawyers handle everything. I can ask them, but I do not guarantee anything."

"You rich people are all alike."

"In fact, I have a very dear friend who has an incurable disease, and the prospects are very dim according to the ophthalmologists. I would like to help him first as it hampers his lifestyle."

"I am sorry to hear that."

"Let me see what the lawyers can do. They have the final say about all my financial matters. It's out of my hands. Considering the extenuating circumstances, they may—and I only say *may*—be able to help your friend."

"I hope a miracle happens to your friend and my close friend."

"I have an appointment. I have to go now. I'm sorry to cut our meeting short. We can go out together."

"Let's keep in touch. Don't be a stranger."

They walked several blocks through cobbled streets, and Georgina greeted her friend in the doorway of a porn shop. Georgina kissed Fiona on the cheek, and they trotted off in opposite directions.

It puzzled Fiona what a dying cancer-stricken emaciated person could be doing in a porn shop but decided it was none of her business. Maybe she went in there to escape the rain, which, although not heavy, threatened to pour. A huge dark cloud hovered in the heavens, but where Fiona stood, a burst of sunlight appeared. She glanced again at the dark clouds and was almost blinded by the light. That was an unusual circumstance, she thought. However, she had to be on her way to the Royal Opera House.

As she trundled to the back door, a heavyset woman in African garb smiled at her and said, "Good afternoon, Ms. Morgan."

"Hello," Fiona replied.

She stood in front of her, obstructing her entrance. The African said, "I come from the darkest region of Africa. Something tells me that evil surrounds you. I am warning you strongly to be careful in every aspect of your life. My words will ring true one day. Be not afraid. I will pray for you." She handed her a card.

Inside the Opera House, the makeup artist applied pale makeup to Fiona's face and neck after she had donned her black drab dress. Hoping that there would be a sizeable crowd, Fiona peeped through the curtain. Sitting in his usual place, Lord Von Pragh seemed to be engrossed in conversation with a dark-haired voluptuous beauty at his side. A rising tide of resentment and envy arose in Fiona.

Who could that gorgeous-looking woman be? Whoever she was, she was extremely exotic looking with lustrous black hair framing a perfectly contoured face and bedazzling eyes. Here was Fiona, thinking that Lord Von Pragh was sincere and belonged to her and her only. Aware that this was London, in a way, she was not surprised. He had the looks, charisma, and wherewithal to have any woman, and why not? Maybe, she thought, she had neglected him of late with her many pursuits, which kept her preoccupied.

It was time to start her performance. Vowing to render a spectacular artist's rendition of Mimi, Fiona would demonstrate to this sloe-eyed other woman that she could do what she could not. Had Lord Von Pragh perhaps found out that she had seen George Gronback, the photographer, resulting in a twinge of jealousy. Self-assured though he may be, perhaps he suffered as a result of agnosia. Was he reverting to his old ways prior to his marriage to Christiana?

Mustering all the courage she could command, Fiona sag the role of Mimi. Although she dedicated it to him, she was unaware that he believed that. The exotic beauty was nestled close to Lord

Von Pragh, causing a stab of jealousy to pierce Fiona's heart. Imagine the gall of him to do it in front of her. Why couldn't he be secretive about it?

The drums were loud, almost causing pain in Fiona's ears. Or was it that she was too sensitive tonight to the situation confronting her? She concentrated on the conductor and his baton, although she found it difficult not to avert her eyes to Lord Von Pragh and the mounting jealousy that rekindled itself as the paramour at his side whispered in his ear. How she wished she were in her place. But she reminded herself that the opera must go on despite the fact that the man she loved was trampling on her feelings. If only she knew the secret of his success with women. Wealth, power, and prestige were significant factors, she knew.

The evening seemed long, and it was with a sigh of relief that the curtain closed on the finale. But not before she saw Lord Von Pragh and his beauty applaud her for quite some time. Fiona wished that she could mesmerize him with her beauty as this woman seemed quite capable of doing. With the applause ringing in her ears, Fiona retreated to her dressing room.

Feeing alone and unloved, she changed into a mufti after removing the heavy pancake makeup. Reminding herself triumphantly that she was scheduled to accompany him to St. Peter Port, her spirit rose. She would have him all to herself for one week. Should she go or should she stay in London? Of course, she would go. This man must be the very fabric of her being.

Consumed with loving him, she vowed this other woman would not come between them. A tear trickled down her cheek at the idea. Oh! What inner torment she felt. Her heart cried out for him while a voice beckoned her to use caution. Which voice should she follow?

This was no time to reason. Fiona was beyond sane reasoning. She was betwixt and between about everything. Totally muddled and confused, she dabbed her eyes. Resolved to go at it alone if need be, she must concentrate on her career. She would not be smitten senseless by this man who had a reputation for bedding and leaving women. Was that all he thought about Fiona? Another conquest in his lifetime? A woman to be discarded at his whim? No. She would not cling to him if he didn't want her. Too much pride would not allow her to do this.

Lord Von Pragh was her first love. This exotic woman seemed to be the epitome of feminine allure. Fiona felt she was a far cry from that. Career oriented, she would have to resort to that to forget him. Although she knew that he was not jealous of her rising career, he must be seeking more attention from Fiona. He had made remarks to that effect before. Why hadn't she listened? What was she to do?

Right now Fiona must go outside, put on a happy face, and keep her adoring, adulating public satisfied by signing autographs. Admittedly, they kept Fiona's ego high. But she was frail—frail in the face of rejection by the man she loved and who occupied her waking and sleeping hours. Perhaps now he was in the throes of his exotic beauty. Why couldn't she be so lucky?

Only the repulsive, obese Rory McCormack was the single man interested in marrying Fiona. She would rather die than wind up with him. Perhaps she was destined to be unlucky in love. There had been moments when she had reached the heights of pleasure and now was wallowing in despair.

Obviously she was no longer a significant other in Lord Von Pragh's life. Fiona had stiff competition, and she didn't like it one iota. Heavy of heart, Fiona was driven home in a limousine. She wished she had the audacity to follow Lord Von Pragh and his companion to his residence or wherever they were going. Maybe they were heading to a club where he would introduce her to his friends and fellow members. Not that he was a gambler, but he liked the night life. Undaunted, she went to her flat. There she flung her clothes on the couch and went to bed.

In a heightened sense of awareness, Fiona heard the phone ringing. Whoever it was, she was in no frame of mind to communicate with anyone. She let the phone ring. What if it were Lord Von Pragh? He would have every reason to suspect that she was out having a good time with one of her many fans. Let it ring, she said to herself. Possessed of pride and stamina, she was not about to subject herself to this onslaught of degradation. This is the only word she could associate with Lord Von Pragh, flaunting this beautiful stranger before her eyes.

Inordinately jealous, Fiona could hardly comprehend the audacity of Lord Von Pragh when he had literally professed his love for her. Maybe he was a two-timer who pulled the same trick on every woman. Yet she thought he was too sensitive to do that. But who could fathom him? Not Fiona. Far too inexperienced, she must learn the thinking of men and the caliber of man she was dealing with. The phone stopped ringing. Turning on her left side, she decided sleep would be the answer.

However, sleep would not come that easily. Fiona wanted Lord Von Pragh at her side even with the interference of Christiana. The latter was preferable to the lady in the Royal Opera House whom she had no doubt could sweep any man off his feet. The question was, Could she actually soar him to unearthly realms as Christiana had? Wouldn't she be nosey enough to strike while the fire was hot than have him enjoy a liaison with this new beauty?

Had Christiana intervened and sought this stranger to prevent Lord Von Pragh's infatuation becoming deeper? It was entirely possible. Anything was in the realm of possibility. Christiana had chosen a desirable woman that most men would literally give their eye tooth just to be seen with her. Stabs of envy wrenched Fiona's heart at the cruelty he had inflicted on her. What a contrast to his previous loving behavior. Was Christiana's venom mounting?

It was strictly a figment of Fiona's imagination that Lord Von Pragh should be jealous of George Gronback. If he even knew the circumstances surrounding their meeting, it would be indeed laughable. The opera sweetheart was no laughing matter. Fiona recognized the attention he showered on her and realized he had meted out the similar treatment to her. What a two-faced cad, she thought.

Then Fiona wished she had taken up the phone and answered it. Now it was too late. The phone was silent. What if she never heard from Lord Von Pragh again? How could she be sure it was him? She was not certain and must face the consequence. Why on earth would he be bothered with Fiona when he could spend the night locked in the embrace of a woman whom Fiona guessed was in high demand by any man's standard? Would he deliver the same drivel to her as he had to Fiona?

Again she asked herself, would Christiana put in her two cents' worth and interfere as she usually did? For once, Fiona hoped it was true. After all, she had endured it much longer than this other woman. Why she had tolerated it for such an inordinate amount of time was a mystery to her. The mystery must end. Let the stranger face similar challenges. She was far too pretty to put up with hindrances to love. Maybe the pretty woman regarded Lord Von Pragh as a debauched sickly man who was not of her caliber. How well did she know him? For how long had he been dating her? Was he two-timing her while Fiona thought blindly that he was in love with her? Lovemaking had not been consummated between Fiona and Lord Von Pragh. Was it the cause of the ever-present Christiana, or the other woman constantly in the background?

Trying to solve the problem was far more perplexing and complicated than Fiona wanted it to be. She meditated, as was her wont, and before long, she was in slumberland. That night she dreamt Lord Von Pragh was holding the elegant and beautifully manicured hands of the femme fatale she had seen at the Opera House. Before long he was luring her to a four-poster tapestry-draped bed and kissing her passionately all over her svelte body. Totally responsive, he was wild with desire.

Then Lord Von Pragh did what Fiona could not under any circumstances accomplish. They made love for what seemed an interminable length of time. It was a passion of such intensity that incensed Fiona. A helmeted policeman stood nearby. Thunder roared in the heavens. Lightning flashed, causing the man on the gargoyle to topple. The horse on which Fiona was riding bolted at such speed that she was thoroughly enjoying herself as she crossed between rivers and streams in a joyful mood. Her hair was lashing against her face. Lord Von Pragh and the femme fatale disappeared. In a park-like setting, a snake the length of which she had never seen before, was coiled around a tall tree.

Fiona heard a distinct female voice say, "We all can't be lucky enough to be Irish, Pat."

That was the end of the dream. Fiona awakened immediately, quite perturbed. What on earth could that dream be interpreted as other than Lord Von Pragh was making love to another woman? Suspicion and envy brought her back to her senses.

Fiona must forget Lord Von Pragh. Dogged by his reputation, she was sure she could never change him. Frankly, that was the last thing she wanted to do. She loved him for himself and for no other reason than she believed he was a good man. No. She could not tolerate the hijinks he put her through. What was far more infuriating was the lady's lasciviousness in the dream. *Lady* was not the term she could use in association with her. *Whore* seemed more in keeping with her lewd behavior in bed.

Yet there was no denying her breeding. Where had the whore polished the many tricks that soared Lord Von Pragh to a nonearthly paradise? Why wasn't Fiona more accomplished in lovemaking? It was a simple fact facing her squarely in the face. Her Ursuline boarding school upbringing enabled her to display her talent on stage when in reality she had no experience with the way of love.

While the lover was amply endowed, Fiona was only thirty-four B bust. That made her jealous. And yet she was satisfied how she looked. Riding on horseback, Fiona would not like her breasts flopping through the river and tributaries she had seen herself in the dream. Cold-bloodedly she reminded herself it was but a dream. Did it have any association with reality?

Maybe an amply endowed woman was far more appealing and feminine looking to Lord Von Pragh. Who knows? All women seemed to be fair game to him. Fiona must banish him from her mind now and forever more.

Her mind in total disarray, she went to the kitchen to toast an English muffin. The door bell rang with such urgency that she let the person in. Let it be Lord Von Pragh, she prayed silently.

"Good morning, my Irish beauty. Thank God you're alive."

"You look all flustered, Charles. What's the matter?"

"What's the matter? Didn't you hear your phone ringing last evening?"

"Oh! It was you. I was tired."

"You sound disappointed."

"I'm terribly sorry, Charles. Come here and let me make you feel welcome."

Fiona threw her arm around him and gave him a big smothering kiss.

"Don't you know this is London?" he said. "Anything can happen in a big metropolis."

"I'll tell you why I didn't answer the phone. Lord Von Pragh had the audacity to come to the Royal Opera House with this smashing lady. Can you believe the nerve of him?"

"Yes. I can."

"What about my feelings, Charles? There I had to perform seething with rage and pretend I didn't care."

"He's a handsome devil. I'm sure he has his share of women. Crème de la crème, I would say."

"Don't remind me, Charles."

"That's what the dating life is all about."

"How many times did you ring, Charles?"

"I can't remember. I gave up. How do you know you didn't miss His Lordship's phone call?"

"I know. I'm just punishing myself."

"Precisely."

"You probably missed out on a wonderful evening of hanky-panky and lovemaking."

"Gosh! I hope not. I didn't tell you a dream I had. Lord Von Pragh was making indescribable love to the femme fatale he was with at the Royal Opera House."

"That was a dream. Forget about dreams. They are merely unfulfilled wishes."

"You answer the phone, Charles, if it rings again."

Barely had she uttered the words when the phone tinkled.

"Hello," Charles said. "Hello," he repeated in a louder tone.

There was a click on the other end. Fiona's heart was going pitter-patter. Could it be Lord Von Pragh? she wondered.

"Stop playing games," Charles said. "Life is too short. Anyway, I'm going home. I'm glad you're all right."

With those words, he was out the door and rushing down the staircase.

Fiona followed to pick up her mail. What joy gladdened her eyes as she opened the one invitation to join Lord Von Pragh on a trip to St. Peter Port. Maybe the femme fatale was not instrumental in exerting her formidable influence over Lord Von Pragh with exciting sex about she had dreamed. No. Fiona had no intention of mentioning what had transpired in the dream. Right now she must finish packing her bag for a holiday with the only man who meant life itself to her.

Eager with anticipation, Fiona was waiting outside her flat, attired in her most alluring outfit, when the driver picked up her suitcase and deposited it in the trunk of the car. Hardly able to suppress her excitement, she could barely suppress the sparkle in her eyes at seeing Lord Von Pragh. As if nothing had happened, she sat beside him. What a warm, fuzzy feeling enveloped her.

"I can't wait to be alone with you," he whispered. "It seemed like an eternity not being in your company."

"Did I miss you?" she replied.

"I thought you were gallivanting with some young buck who had swept you off your feet. It's not a difficult happening in this exciting city."

Taking her hand in his warm embrace sent shivers of thrills throughout her body. This cannot be, she reminded herself. Here she was, competing with one of the most exotic beauties that graced the streets of London, and it was she, Fiona Morgan, at his side. Feeling like a celebrated debutante, she basked in the luxury. It seemed like no length of time before they arrived at Southampton dock.

Seagulls circled and squawked overhead. Policemen were plentiful, with police cars flashing everywhere. Getting out of the car, the mist hit Fiona on the skin and frizzed her hair.

Over the intercom, a voice said, "Attention, please, ladies and gentlemen. There will be no more departures to Guernsey, Jersey, Alderney, and Sark due to an outbreak of measles. It's a safety concern. Passengers will be reimbursed for the inconvenience."

"Measles!" Lord Von Pragh exclaimed. "I don't want to contact that. I'm looking forward to having children one day. I know it can cause a man to become sterile."

He smiled a knowing smile as he glanced directly into Fiona's eyes. Despite the seriousness of the announcement, she was happier than she had been for the last week. Was that a reference that he wanted to marry her and have children? Yet he was such a complex character that she didn't know how to fathom him. True. He was her soul mate, and yet his behavior made her question the validity of his remark.

Arm in arm they walked downhill to a nearby wharf bar and grill where they had a seafood sandwich.

"Where are we heading now?" Fiona enquired.

"We'll find something. The driver is on his way home, which leaves us no choice but to stay in one of the hotels."

Her mind racing with excitement, she said, "Will I still be your nurse?"

"Of course. Could I find a prettier nurse than you here?"

Holding Fiona's elbow, she carried her suitcase while he struggled with his luggage plus his cane with crowds of people walking in every direction. Finding it impossible to get an empty taxi, they walked several blocks on the boulevard near the ocean. Eventually they labored uphill slowly in search of a hotel room. Every hotel and bed and breakfast had a sign: "No Vacancy." Did the low, mournful cry of the foghorn in the distance herald the voice of Christiana beckoning him to Bedford Castle?

"You're special, my darling," he said with a touch of tenderness. "I'll take you to one of my favorite hotels here in Southampton."

Not without a certain degree of cynicism did she wonder how many other lovers had stayed with him there too.

"Good. I'm exhausted," she said, "as you must be from walking."

After a long trek, they arrived at Atlantic House, which in bygone days had been a refuge for sailors. Lord Von Pragh explained that it had been converted to Atlantic House, where everybody who is anybody stayed. It was also the hotel where several passengers of the ill-fated *Titanic* had stayed on the eve of their departure.

"I'm superstitious, Robert. Let's go elsewhere."

"You see for yourself better than I can that every bed and breakfast and hotel are full."

"It's against my better nature. All right, you're tired." She gave him a sympathetic look.

Arriving at Atlantic House, a desk clerk came forward while they were waiting on the queue.

"Your Lordship," he said, "there are no more rooms or suite. However, a kindly young man is willing to give you his room. It's small but adequate under the circumstances."

"Who is this man?"

"A protestor, he says, who knows of you participating in the poll tax demonstration in London."

"That is very kind. Please write his name down for me."

"He wishes to remain anonymous. He said one good deed deserves another."

"I'm sure I'll see him again. Tell him if ever I can be of assistance, to contact me through Parliament."

The hotel clerk led the way to the elevator past an open door parlor where patrons played cards while a porter put their luggage on a cart. He switched the light on in the room.

"Be my lover. Be my nurse while we are together," Lord Von Pragh said.

"Why? Where are you going?"

Fiona could only surmise that he wouldn't be back in the arms of the other woman when they returned to London. Or would it be with Christiana in spirit? Had he stayed here with his beloved wife on occasions? Maybe he wanted to relive precious moments with her when she was alive and vibrant and oozing with sex appeal. Thinking inwardly, she vowed to make this an unforgettable time. Who knows? This might be her last date with him.

"Please sit on the bed, Robert, while I undress you," she teased.

She leaned the cane against the nearby wall. Gently she removed his coat and jacket.

"Come here," he said, hugging her towards him as he lay down on the bed. "You remind me of my wonderful mother, who catered to my every whim. I miss her constantly."

"I realize that with every passing day. If I become too demanding with you, let me know in no uncertain terms."

She bent down and removed his shoes and socks. Tickling his foot, he withdrew his leg and pulled her up on the bed. With his hot, wet tongue, he probed her mouth, lighting a fire within her such as she had never known. With a response that she knew not from whence it originated, her body tingled with every movement. Feeling his loins tighten, he breathed into her ear. Fiona sensed that she was in another world, a world where there was no danger, no envy, just cocooned in his arms. The long muscular curves of his body pressed against hers so that she felt at one with him.

Fiona wanted to feel the rugged manliness of his skin, to inhale the scent that he exuded from every pore. Slowly she unbuttoned his shirt, one button at a time.

"I want to talk seriously to you now, Fiona. If I were to ask you to marry me, what would you say?"

Silent for what seemed an eternity, she said, "I have to think it over."

"I would save you from the many suitors and young bucks who adore you."

"I love you very much, but I had a dream about you that unnerved me."

"Tell me your dream."

"I didn't mention it to you because I didn't get a chance. Bringing a gorgeous female to the Royal Opera house was very disturbing. But what I saw both of you doing in the dream was very upsetting."

"I didn't think someone as beautiful as you could be jealous. But they say beautiful women are very insecure. Is it because I suffer from an incurable disease that you wouldn't marry me?"

"Quite the contrary." She kissed him with such fervor that must have sent him reeling.

"I know you can cure me of my visual agnosia."

"Believe me, I've tried. So far, it hasn't worked."

"But I keep dreaming that I can see again, and my visual agnosia is no more."

"Anything you believe can happen, although this would be a miracle."

"Forget about me. Tonight I want you to hit the high notes. You do it on stage, which drives me wild. I almost have an orgasm in my seat. Do it with me in bed."

"It excites me to think about it."

"Let's have some wine to relax."

Lord Von Pragh picked up the phone and ordered. Twenty minutes later, the bell boy walked in with two bottles of French Pomerol Petrus on ice. He decanted the wine into sparkling crystal glasses.

"Cheers! To my darling, Fiona," Lord Von Pragh said.

"Slainte!" she said, toasting him.

Linked arm in arm, they sipped the wine, slowly savoring each sip.

He said, "I want to let it all hang out tonight."

Having uttered those words, he kissed her cheek, sending waves of rapture throughout her body. Squirming and sighing, she let out a satin-like moan. Feeling giddy with imbibing the wine, he pushed his body against hers so that she thought she would swoon.

Relieved that she was lying down, Fiona kissed his neck, making him respond with such a fierceness that she was almost afraid, not of him, but of her own reaction to a man that must be hers forever. Why must she sacrifice herself to a man utterly and completely when she was likely to be hurt? But that was not what was on her mind now as she savored every kiss, every nuance, the slightest movement that exalted her beyond no return.

Fiona spied a black fleeting shadow on the sandpapered wall. She thought about the writing on the wall. This was different. There was an ominous sinister quality about it. What did it imply? Did it implicate her and Lord Von Pragh? The latter ignited a fire in her that could not be quenched, the embers of which were still smoldering. Not by separation, not by time, not by the femme fatale, and not even by the spirit of Christiana could sever the bond between them.

Fiona kissed him with a love and intensity that she was sure equaled that of Christiana.

Lord Von Pragh kissed Fiona's breast, making her more aroused. She wanted to nurture him, to fulfill his every need. She asked herself if that was possible. If not, she would come close to it. In between sips of wine, Fiona felt totally relaxed. He moved down her abdomen, relishing that soft, supple skin. She pushed him down further, spreading her legs involuntarily.

"Come to me. Come to me," he whispered.

Fiona thrust her body to him with an abandon that was foreign to her. Kissing the inner aspect of her thighs, she cradled his head towards her. Relishing the warmth of his tongue and the sensations it aroused within her, she felt this is the moment. Releasing soft intermittent moans, she was rudely interrupted by a loud thud on the door.

"Open up. Police!" a booming voice said.

"You've got to help me, Robert," Fiona said in a hushed voice as her heart pounded.

She huddled near him, tears streaming down her face.

"Why? What have you done?"

"Police!" again rang through the door.

After some fumbling, she heard a key turn in the lock. A hand reached in and snapped the chain off the inside door. Stark naked, she stood at the bedside while Lord Von Pragh seemed dazed. The policeman entered.

"Are you Fiona Morgan?"

"Yes, officer."

"You are under arrest as a runaway from Ireland. Get dressed. Who is this bloke with you?"

"I am Lord Robert Von Pragh."

"I'm very sorry for intruding like this, Your Lordship," the policeman said.

"What are the charges against Ms. Morgan?"

"Firstly, she is a runaway. Secondly, she is accused of moral turpitude. There may be other charges pending. That's it for now."

Casting an imploring glance at Lord Von Pragh, she left. Escorted by the policeman, she was led outdoors while several guests gawked at her. Outside in the brisk mist, her hair billowed round her shoulders.

The policeman said, "Turn around. Put your hands behind your back."

Hands cuffed, he escorted her into the black maria. With lights flashing, Fiona arrived at the police station. Inside the precinct were several people, including among them was her worst nightmare, Rory McCormack, who was standing with a detective. The sight of him caused Fiona to panic.

"Where am I going?" Fiona muttered.

"You're going on the next plane to Ireland. You will be met by your guardian so that you will be safe."

Feeling nauseated, she said, "I have to go to the bathroom."

"Let's go." He pushed her roughly, almost causing her to stumble. There she threw up violently with sweat pouring from her face so that she thought she would faint.

Wiping her forehead with the back of her hand, in a faltering voice, she said, "May . . . I call . . . my lawyer, please?"

"Yes. You can make one phone call."

"You'll have to release my hands."

"I'll call. You're cunning enough to run away and elude the law for several months. What's the number?"

"Offhand, I don't know."

"I can't contact the lawyer if you don't know. Come on."

A taxi pulled up by the policeman. With steely determination, Lord Von Pragh emerged with Fiona's suitcase and handbag.

He said, "Ms. Morgan needs her belongings. She is entitled to them."

"Yes, milord," the policeman said.

Tears streaming down her cheeks, Fiona kissed Lord Von Pragh and said, "I don't know if I'll ever see you again."

"I'm going to start working on the matter immediately." Lord Von Pragh walked away in a desolate mood while the police sped away to the airport.

How could this happen? Fiona asked herself. The African sorceress outside the Royal Opera House had warned her, and foolishly she had ignored the advice. She had no one to blame but herself. Could there be a more sinister force at work? Was it the spirit of Christiana ensuring that no one would have Lord Von Pragh?

Passengers of Aer Lingus plane were boarding. Fiona ascended the steps and sat in one of the seats beside an elderly man. The door closed, and the plane took off. It seemed no length of time—perhaps forty-five minutes—when they arrived at Shannon Airport. There she was, Fiona's guardian, waiting for her, accompanied by a man who appeared to be six feet and four inches tall, rather handsome, in a rough kind of way.

"Come on then," the guardian said. "What were you thinking about running away like that?"

"I can't tell you now, but I will one day."

"How did you survive in London? How did you support yourself?"

"I managed. I got a job."

"The mayor, Rory, was so worried about you. I don't know when he first took a notion to you. Of course, you've blossomed into a lovely young woman. It's not me he's interested in. It's you." There was a spiteful, cynical look in her eyes.

"You can have him any day. He's not my cuppa tea."

"You mean that?"

"I swear by my father in heaven."

"It's good to know. I've wasted the best years of my life with this rogue. Here I am getting older each year, and now I can call myself an old spinster."

"You might be just as well off. Sometimes we don't know how lucky we are in present circumstances."

They arrived at the home, which Fiona had known since she attended the Ursuline boarding school. Like her old self, the guardian served tea and soda bread. After she had finished, she went to a small round bottle and, with trembling hands, took out a small white tablet.

"This I'm taking for my nerves. I can't tolerate all the turmoil Rory has put me through since you left. He blames me for you running away. I told him many times it wasn't my fault, but he would have none of it."

"This place is so insular. Everybody knows everybody's business. I loved England."

"What's to become of me? I'm getting old, losing my looks, and I have this Rory coming and going when he feels like it. I give in to him because I have no one else. Everybody is afraid of crossing him."

"It's natural that you are upset. I'm terribly tired. I'm going to bed. Good night."

"Good night. Don't get up to any monkey business."

Feeling the weight of the world on her shoulders, Fiona went upstairs. She noticed there was a bell on the doorknob, which chimed when she opened it. Dog tired and bone weary, all she could think of was Lord Von Pragh. What was he doing tonight? Would he take care of matters and get her back to London?

Ready to shed a tear, she resolved to trust his parting words. It was possible that he was thinking of her. Out of loneliness, would he resort to the femme fatale? Fiona would miss the sophistication and excitement of London. She didn't know why, but the apparition of her grandmother came vividly to her mind. She must not despair.

Young, alive, and healthy, the world would be Fiona's oyster again. In her mind's eye, she sent Lord Von Pragh a healing, and thought she detected a smile on his face. Was that directed towards her? She believed so. But then it could be the femme fatale that brought such joy to his countenance or perhaps Christiana in Bedford Castle. She had no way of knowing for sure. Uncertainty lurked at every twist and turn.

Could Fiona trust her guardian? It was quite a relief to know that she had not relinquished fanciful notions about Rory McCormack. What if he came here while her guardian was away and forced her to marry him? Perish the thought. By hook or by crook, she would never be betrothed to him. He may have pulled the wool over her guardian's eyes, but not Fiona's. Lord Von Pragh was the only man she would consider marrying. Now she was sorry that she had left him in the lurch, when in a halfhearted way he had asked her to marry him.

If Lord Von Pragh were by her side at the moment, Fiona would unequivocally say yes. After all, he had his pride and was not likely to ask her again. Wounded once was enough. She could drop a hint at an opportune time, but would he respond to it? He was a supersensitive man. God knows what it did to his ego.

Lovelorn, Fiona must make the best of her current situation. Reminiscing about his tender touch and suave manner was enough for now to keep her spirit up. Seconds later, she was down in the dumps, wondering if she would ever see him again. Why must life be so troubled? Why did she ever meet Lord Von Pragh? It was a dire situation wherein he had helped her escape the clutches of Rory McCormack and must do it again. From across the Atlantic, she gave him a kiss and imagined him welling a longing that could traverse the ocean.

CHAPTER 18

"Now that you're here, Rory McCormack is giving a Halloween party, and he wants you to be there. I'm going to attend," said the guardian.

"I'm in no mood to go to a party," Fiona replied.

"This is going to be spectacular. Come. I don't want to go on my own. Besides, he wants you more than me to attend."

"There isn't much else going on in Limerick. OK. I'll go with you. Remember, though, you are with Rory McCormack."

"That's if he'll want me."

'Twas the eve of the full moon and Halloween to boot. Downstairs in the parlor, Fiona met her guardian decked out as a bumblebee in yellow fluttering wings. Fiona felt rather drab as a witch with a low-cut black dress, long black gloves, pointed nose, and shrivelled cheekbones. If only Lord Von Pragh were here, she thought. But no, he was not. She would have to confront the gruff and repulsive Rory McCormack. She was sure he would be surrounded by admirers by virtue of the fact that he was the lord mayor of Limerick. Lacking in social graces, women would be attracted to him because of the power and prestige he wielded. Not so Fiona.

Lord Von Pragh was her special person, and nobody could stand between them. Hampered by visual agnosia, Fiona knew he was destined to be her man. There simply was too big a comparison between Lord Von Pragh and Rory McCormack, the former, refined, cultured, and handsome, the latter coarse, who could not attract a fly were it not for the fact he was a politician.

The latter dispatched a limousine for Fiona and her guardian. Outside the entrance was a sign that read "Haunted Hill Insane

Asylum 1017." Inside were chains dangling from the ceiling, a unit of blood in a plastic container attached to a man's arm, a man with a gun pointed at an unsuspecting creature, lunatics behaving erratically in crazy poses, and guards standing by in protective gear.

Fiona and her guardian sat side by side, almost huddled against the onslaught of abnormal beings.

"We are gathered here tonight to celebrate a very special occasion. Let's all be happy tonight with the announcement of the engagement of Rory McCormack, lord mayor of Limerick, to Fiona Morgan."

Silent for several seconds during which time the blood drained from her face, the guardian said, "Ms. Morgan, come up here on stage for Rory McCormack to present you with the ring, which has been handed down from his illustrious great-grandmother."

Looking quizzical, Fiona stammered, "There must be a mistake . . . I'm sure he meant you."

"No. He has a mind of his own. You never know how these politicians think."

"That's it," the guardian said emphatically. "Go on up."

Wending her way through the seated crowd, Fiona neither looked to the right or to the left. A ghostly man with his hands extended appeared to be looking for succor. If only Lord Von Pragh were here to sweep her away from this ugly scene. Now Fiona would be in the bad graces of her guardian as well as being repulsed by a man who seemed more treacherous than the lunatics who decorated the hall. She simply must refuse to become engaged to Rory McCormack. Would he seek revenge if she embarrassed him in front of such a large gathering? He was known to be vengeful, but why should she succumb to the wiles of a politician? They had a reputation to be worse than crooks with the morals of alley cats.

Rory McCormack took her hand at the steps of the stage as Fiona was almost blinded by tears. He led her across the stage with chains dangling from the ceiling, a unit of blood hanging up with nets, which she thought could ensnare her.

Applause started and continued for about five minutes, while Fiona watched the beady eyes of Rory McCormack pierce the very depths of her soul. Silence ensued while he lowered his hand to stifle the crowd.

"As a public figure," the lord mayor said, "I thought I would invite my friends and associates to witness this special occasion. May I present Fiona Morgan with this engagement ring, which has been handed down by my great-grandmother."

Fiona did not extend her hand.

"Let me have your hand," he said, impatience betraying him.

"He's too old for her," a nearby guest said. "She' very pretty and can have any man she wants."

"His girlfriend of many years must be very upset." Guests stared in her guardian's direction.

"The dirty blaggard," a man said within earshot of Fiona.

Rory McCormack took Fiona's hand almost savagely. He put the ring on the third finger of her left hand, which to Fiona looked like a poor man's ring. Not that she cared about that, but it was the giver. Looming over her, he bent down and kissed her perfunctorily on the cheek. Repulsed by it, she wiped the saliva off her face.

Toasting her with a glass of champagne, he said, "To my future bride, Ms. Fiona Morgan. May we be blessed with many children when we marry."

On hearing those words, Fiona burst out crying. Rushing off stage, she retreated to the seat that she had occupied. Gasps of oohs and aahs came from the audience. Fiona did not care one iota. This farcical drama was absolutely unbelievable. If only Lord Von Pragh were here to rescue her.

"My fiancée has been overcome by emotion," said Rory McCormack. "Let's give her time to compose herself."

But compose herself Fiona did not.

"That's your boyfriend of many years. I don't want to snatch him away from you."

"You have," the guardian said.

"But I don't want him or his ring. Take it." She handed over the ring to her guardian.

"I don't want to be accused of stealing."

"No. I stand by what I've said."

"Bless your heart. You know I've always loved Rory. I've stood by him through thick and thin. But you're young and beautiful. Age has passed me by."

There were stares from many tables as Fiona passed the ring to her guardian. Still drinking the champagne, Rory seemed to be in another world with a thirty-something woman at his side, hugging and kissing her. Fiona believed he hardly knew who she was. But she was concise and precise about whom she wanted by her side. It was definitely Lord Von Pragh, not the inebriated Rory McCormack. She must flee this situation as soon as humanly possible. To whom could she turn?

Inordinately jealous without justification, Fiona's guardian could not be trusted. Or could she? She was unaware that there existed a man in Fiona's life who meant everything to her. She would seek the help of her nemesis. She had loved Rory McCormack for so many years. At this point, it was a love-hate relationship. She was not about to lose Rory over a woman half her age.

As she had understood, the guardian's options were limited, whereas the world was Fiona's oyster. Should they be in cahoots to initiate her escape? Did she even need her? By that time, Fiona had escaped, given the ring to her guardian so that she would not be accused of theft, and the fact authenticated by her father's lawyers who had been in the front row during the presentation of the engagement ring. Why had they not come to her rescue when they were aware that she was not in love with Rory McCormack? It seemed like a tragic comedy. Ring or no ring, Fiona was not about to commit herself to a man she hardly knew, let alone about to marry. Why the rush?

Lord Von Pragh must deliver her. No time must be wasted. Time was of the essence. Fiona was certain that her guardian would be happy to see her back in London. She must face the consequences with Rory McCormack. If need be, she would live with Lord Von Pragh. Outlandish though it may seem, it was her only recourse to escape the clutches of the wily politician. With that resolve in mind, she would devise a means of escape.

Fiona had read that it was possible to make herself invisible and wished she could accomplish that feat. For some inexplicable reason, she visualized the stone Lord Von Pragh had given her when they first met. Was it within the realm of normalcy that this stone possessed unique powers? She wondered if she was communicating with Lord Von Pragh. Of this she knew, she was communicating with him telepathically.

Her mind told Fiona to wait. She must follow her heart. She was scheduled to perform at the Royal Opera House in Covent Garden next week. If she did not make an appearance, it probably would be the end of her assignment. Everything she had hoped and dreamed about would be all for naught. Mostly what she worried about was Lord Von Pragh. Would he resort to the femme fatale companion now that Fiona was no longer available? If only she had listened to the African sorceress, would she have wound up in this mess?

The stone, emblazoned with prisms of varying hues, appeared before Fiona's eyes, almost dazzling her. She had always kept it in her handbag. Now she was communing with Lord Von Pragh. Slowly and gingerly she rose from her bed. She retrieved the stone, which had been excavated from the Egyptian ruins. She had always known that stones had specific powers. Holding the stone fearfully in her palm, it emitted an energy that did not seem of this world. In the semidarkness of the room, it glowed with an nonearthly sensation. Did it perhaps have a special energy and could lead her in the right direction? Lying on her back in bed, it appeared around the neck of a sorrowful woman. What was the reason for her angst?

Fiona knew the cause of her own dire situation. She was in despair for Lord Von Pragh, the Royal Opera House, and the delights and vibrancy of London. Would Lord Von Pragh be able to rescue her? She must devise her own extrication.

Almost as if she were awake, Fiona saw Lord von Pragh in a semitrance state. Holding the stone in her palm, she saw her feet becoming invisible as she trundled across the airport tarmac. A brilliant purple orb appeared before her. Yes. He was helping her. But there must be no mistake. The energy radiating from the stone and under Lord Von Pragh's direction, Fiona was becoming invisible. The energy gradually spiraled upwards so that she was totally invisible. Was this her imagination or wishful thinking? Something like this had never happened to her before. Was she in a heightened state of trance? Feeling as if she were surrounded by fire, Fiona realized that she had reached an exalted state of invisibility. It was not as difficult as she had assumed. Was her grandmother helping her too? Feeling a hand guiding her, she could not fathom the guiding hand. Spirit guides were known to have achieved miraculous results in difficult circumstances. That it should happen to Fiona was nothing short of a miracle. Lord Von Pragh dissolved into the mist.

Drifting off to sleep, Fiona tried to duplicate the invisibility scene. However, the stone fell out of her hand, and before long, she was fast asleep. Her dream was of Lord Von Pragh living in opulent circumstances while entertaining the femme fatale who had accompanied him to the Royal Opera House. She was wearing a wedding ring, which incensed Fiona. Her voice had become constricted, and she became so tongue-tied that she could not sing. She saw a diplomat in another room with a little boy.

Trying to decipher the dream was of little consequence. It was but a dream, she told herself. What if it were true? Fiona must banish such crazy notions from her mind. Persist they did even though she was sure Lord Von Pragh loved her. Of course, he was capable of wooing more than one woman. Who could resist the femme fatale? Fiona wished she could be as alluring as her. She was not, and it caused her great anxiety as she moped about in her guardian's house. She must practice becoming invisible so that she could escape from Ireland and the evil influence of Rory McCormack. Doubt beset her about the effectiveness of becoming invisible at the right time. It worked for her once. Would it be effective when she needed it most?

By hook or by crook, Fiona was intent on escaping. She might have to resort to added measures to achieve that end. She wanted to be with the man she loved and was destined to marry. Two lonely souls needed each other.

However, there were many other factors that must be taken into consideration. Would the invisibility work outdoors? This was a very important aspect of the stone. Could it be affected by the elements?

She must keep it next to her skin? Would extreme cold matter? How about her state of mind? Here were so many questions whirring around in her head. She must not think negatively but have a very positive attitude. Would her grandmother be holding her hand, guiding her safely to the desired destination?

Would the position of the moon be significant? What if Saturn and Uranus, the planets of the unexpected, were present? What if Fiona lost the stone in the dark? Last, but not least, if Christiana interfered. She was definitely trouble. Was she still not at peace? There was no end to the unforeseen circumstances that could rear its head at the last minute.

For the next three nights, Fiona practiced becoming invisible. Sometimes it worked better than others. Now she must get down to brass tacks. There was no end to the bitterness and hatred expressed by Fiona's guardian. Naturally, it was Fiona who was blamed for alienation of affection. She wished she could get it into her guardian's head that there simply was no chemistry between Rory McCormack and Fiona. But Lord Von Pragh. That was another matter. Even though parted by the Atlantic Ocean, oftentimes she felt she was communicating in the flesh.

On occasions, when her guardian had an extra nip of whiskey, she became so enraged that Fiona thought she would have a stroke. Her lips and hands would tremble, and she would raise the glass to Fiona.

"It's all your fault," she would say. "But you won't be young forever. The same dirt he dished out to me, he will do to you. Is it any wonder I have to see the doctor and take nerve pills after all the years I've wasted on him?"

"I honestly can understand your predicament. I'd like to get the hell out of here too."

"Who is stopping you?"

"I'm a virtual prisoner in this house with a gong on the doorknob."

"Ach! Take no notice of that."

"You know my comings and goings."

"I'm only doing my job for that worthless bastard, the lord mayor. I've never been able to do anything without him and his cronies finding out. When you were away at boarding school, he worshipped the ground I walked on. Maybe I've let my appearance go through too much drinking. Look at me. Have I?"

"You don't look any the worst for wear in my eyes."

"You can't trust a woman to tell the truth."

"Have I ever lied to you?"

"Begorrah! I think not. How was I to know? I was stewed to the gills at times. I'll forget him." There was a steely determination in her voice.

"You may be lonely now. You'll find another man."

"You wouldn't marry him and let me be the scorn of the city of Limerick? He must have been off at the race track every day that I haven't seen him. A bad habit, that gambling."

"I never knew he gambled."

"He'd bet on anything. Horses, cards, the stock market, you name it. Sometimes he doesn't have a pot to piss in. Out of nowhere he would have money again. I can't make head or tail of him."

"You're too good for him."

"He doesn't think so." She swigged back a shot of whiskey. "Between you and me, he's up to no good."

"What do you mean?"

"I feel it in my bones. He's very cagey. It spooks me at times. Keep that under your belt."

"Is it any wonder you have to take tranquillizers?"

"I don't know where I'd be without them."

"As long as they help you, continue taking them."

"You might change your mind about marrying him if you knew as much as I do."

"Take my word for it. There'll be no marriage to the mayor of Limerick."

"I'd like to put a little sense into your head."

As her guardian fumbled her way upstairs to her bedroom, all Fiona could think of was Lord Von Pragh. Wasn't it a pity that her guardian couldn't enlighten her about Lord Von Pragh? The sooner

Fiona fled Limerick, the better. Anything was possible. The handsome aristocratic profile appeared before her eyes as she plotted her escape. She imagined herself cozied up to him before a roaring fire at his flat.

Delighted to help him, she would cater to his every whim and sexual fantasy.

Maybe it wasn't such a good idea to schedule a ride to the airport with the driver her guardian had used. Fiona's baggage was light. When the gas lamp lighter did his gloaming rounds, she would ask him for help and make arrangements for a ride to the airport. Christmas was but a month away. Darkness shrouded the countryside early. There was a chill in the air. The streetlamp lighter appeared like clockwork each evening. He was known to be a reliable man with a wife and eight children.

Noticing that she was becoming increasingly depressed, Fiona urged her guardian to take a nip of whiskey.

"I will," she said, "if you join me."

"Sit down. Let me get it for you. You need someone special to lighten your life."

"It's gloomy with the days so short. I feel lonelier than ever with Christmas looming."

While her guardian sat in the parlor, listening to a talk show, Fiona brought in two drinks. She handed her a stiff whiskey to which she had added ten milligrams of Valium. Guilt ridden, she watched her guardian smack her lips as she downed the first gulp.

"God forgive me," she said silently as she raised her glass. "This is a nice, smooth vodka."

The water straight from the stone well minus the vodka was refreshing. Fiona had to have all her wits about her. Vodka was out of the question.

"I feel guilty feeling so good after a few nips of this."

While Fiona's mind was as clear as a bell, a clock in the nearby belfry tolled.

"What time is it?" she muttered incoherently.

"Five."

She let out a huge yawn and languished in the chair, saying, "I feel like a snooze."

Her guardian took another gulp as Fiona's stomach churned with the prospect of the consequences of her action. She was used to taking five milligrams of Valium at night instead of ten. It made her drowsy, and it couldn't possibly kill her. She would be none the wiser in the morning when she awakened. Overwhelmed with guilt, Fiona added a little more whiskey in case her guardian needed it, so that she would not have to get up from her seat. Fiona's hand trembled, but she told herself it was her only choice.

Fiona peered out into the darkness. There were no houses within half a mile radius. Any minute now the lamp lighter would climb the pole. With her bag in one hand and the stone Lord Von Pragh had given her, she dashed across the darkened street. Suddenly the light went on.

"Good evening, Joe."

"It's you, Fiona."

"Yes."

"Haven't seen you in a long time. Home for Christmas, eh?"

"I have to leave tonight from Shannon Airport."

"You're a brave one travelling alone."

"I have a big favor to ask you, Joe. Could you possibly give me a ride to the airport? I'll make it worth your while."

Joe's kind eyes brightened, and his ruddy cheeks broadened into a wide smile under the glowing gas lamp. He said, "Every little bit helps for Christmas. When you have your wee ones, you'll realize that."

Immediately Fiona thought of Lord Von Pragh. If only his vision could be restored like the gas lamp illuminating the darkness. Her heart ached for him with an insurmountable longing. She must reach him quickly. Faltering footsteps interrupted her thoughts. Fiona jumped with a surprising alacrity.

"That's the little tinker boy emptying the chamber pot," Joe said. "He does it when the light goes on. I think he's afraid of the dark."

Such a wide-eyed gaze he portrayed that Fiona felt sorry for him.

"Do you have a copper, miss. Sorry I scared you."

Gladly Fiona gave him two shiny half crowns. Such delight lit up his sorrowful eyes that it made Fiona's heart light.

"Maybe you brought me and my friend good luck," Fiona said.

"I'll pray tonight that you have the best of times. Thank you. Thank you, miss." He scampered into the fields with the wind whistling in the treetops towards the caravan, his eyes dancing like stars in the moonlight.

If only Lord Von Pragh could look as happy as this with eyes full of sparkle and life. Could this little tinker boy bring him luck? It was entirely possible. If two half crowns could bring such happiness to him, she was sure he would say a little prayer for her and Lord Von Pragh that night. She believed that this little frightened tinker who had so little could give so much more than he received. She was sure that God answered the prayers of the forlorn and the forgotten of this world.

"I have a few more gas lamps to light," Joe said. "I can do it in my sleep. Hop in."

Fiona seated herself in the front seat. They were off with Joe, lighting the gas lamps on the way. It seemed an eternity before they reached the airport.

"You can leave me here," Fiona said as she gathered her few belongings.

She handed the driver ten pounds, and he was off, bidding her good-bye and a heartfelt thank you. The airport was not crowded. Fiona went to the counter and bought her ticket to Gatwick airport. Before long she was on the plane. In a matter of forty-five minutes, she arrived in London, breathing a sigh of relief. Holding the stone in her hand, she hailed a taxi to her flat, every now and then glancing furtively behind her. Would the police be searching for her? she wondered.

All was still within and without as Fiona opened the door to her flat. The stillness was interrupted by the ringing of the phone. When she picked it up, there was silence on the other end. Maybe it was the Royal Opera House cancelling her appearance. After all, she had disappeared without a trace. Waiting for the water to boil, she mulled over in her head who the mystery person on the other end of the phone could be. Was someone tracing her footsteps? Telling herself that she must not be paranoid, she sat by the phone, sipping a cup of Earl Grey tea. She was not hungry. When the phone rang again, she jumped in her chair.

"Hello!" she said.

It was the magical voice of Lord Von Pragh that sent shivers of delight throughout her body and thrilled her beyond words, leaving her speechless for a few moments.

"Fiona, my darling! How did you manage to dodge your suitor?"

"By magic, and it worked."

"I think you should stay at my flat in the mews till this situation has blown over."

"I'm mentally exhausted. Do you have room for me?"

"Of course. Do you want to come tonight?"

"I think I'll be safe. I've learnt to become invisible with your magic stone."

"You have to give a performance tomorrow. I called the director of music and assured him that you would be there. He gasped a sigh of relief when I told him."

"Will you be in the audience, Robert?"

"I wouldn't miss it for the world. Darling! I've missed you more than I can say."

"I thought I'd be hemmed in Limerick forever. I vowed to escape to be once more in your loving arms. That swine, Rory McCormack, embarrassed me by inviting me to a Halloween party. He called me up on stage to present me with a cheap engagement ring. There were so many people and constituents in attendance that I had to accept it. Needless to say, that didn't sit well with my guardian, who was livid with him. He has the audacity to think that I'm going to marry him."

"What are you going to do with this fraudster?"

"I'm in a dilemma. I think I'll ask Charles Phelps for Dubois to protect me. His Jack Russell terrier mutt is so smart he'll put up a ruckus. He's able to elude anyone who tries to catch him."

"Are you going to do it tonight?"

"Yes."

"I hope Dubois remembers me and doesn't try to bite my leg off."

"He's as smart as a whip. He loves you as much as I do. There is no more loyal friend than a dog who has been rescued from the pound."

"I hope I can prove to be as loyal as Dubois."

"You always have. I'll say good night and be on my way to Charles Phelps's house. I can't wait to see you tomorrow."

Fiona decided she would walk there as the evening was brisk with russet leaves carpeting the pavements. Dubois greeted Fiona like a long-lost relative. He jumped on her and smothered kisses all over her face. Having related the nightmare of the Limerick scene, Charles Phelps agreed to loan Dubois to Fiona.

"Dubois has a sweet disposition," Charles said, "but I think, if push came to shove, he would prove to be a guard dog. Always on the alert, he has a very strong sixth sense. Try and catch him, it's like trying to find a needle in a hay stack. He's as good as any German shepherd. Nobody can catch Dubois if he doesn't want to be caught."

"You can trust me with Dubois. I'll treat him well."

"I know you will. Besides, he trusts women more than men. The parrot is going to miss him. Leave the music on for him. It soothes his restless spirit."

Fiona put the leash on Dubois. He was very excited as she led him down the street back to her flat. After he had sniffed every nook and cranny, he made himself at home on the couch, listening to the strains of Mozart. He had his toys and seemed quite preoccupied with them.

Let any stranger come to the door, Fiona thought. She and her companion dog were prepared for them. That night she slept well. However, she did have a perplexing, though quite unfathomable dream, before she awakened.

Fiona recalled that she was in an operating room. She saw an intellectual ophthalmologist doing surgery on the eyes of someone with very fine instruments. She walked by. She heard Lord Von Pragh screaming as he was being excruciatingly tortured.

He was writhing and screaming, "Let me go! Let me go!"

Someone said, "He did all kinds of things in Amsterdam."

The room was in semidarkness. People outside were shocked at what was transpiring. Lord Von Pragh was still screaming when Fiona woke up.

What on earth could this dream mean? she wondered. Lord Von Pragh had never been operated on for his psychic agnosia. He had been informed by every ophthalmologist that there was no cure for psychic agnosia. Because it was so rare and psychosomatic in origin, it was not likely that research would not be initiated for its cure. More disturbing was the excruciating torture Lord Von Pragh was enduring.

Why the plaintive, pleading cry of "Let me go. Let me go"?

What was he referring to? Did he want Fiona to release him from the bondage of love? He never gave any inclination in that direction. Yet his blindness had initiated after the death of Christiana. Was she still clinging to him? Did he always feel her presence?

Was it safe for Fiona to assume that Lord Von Pragh had reached the end of his tether? Was he asking Christiana to release him from his psychic agnosia and the subsequent limits it imposed on his lifestyle? Would she help him? Fiona knew that one day he would be a normal man again without limitations. How it would be accomplished was a complete mystery to her. Her faith in the supernatural was strong. She must pray to her spirit guides, particularly to her grandmother, to restore vision to the man for whom she would do anything.

Back at the Royal Opera House on that drizzly cold evening, Fiona greeted Lord Von Pragh in the dressing room. She could hardly believe her luck at the sight of him. He kissed with such ardor that Fiona thought she would faint at the tumult it aroused within her. Her passions afire, she pressed her body savagely against his that she wanted to have sex there and then.

Reluctantly he pulled away, saying, "I don't want to spoil your pancake makeup. We'll celebrate tonight. I know a dive of a nightclub I would like to introduce you to. I think you'll like it."

Going on stage in a euphoric mood, Fiona couldn't help but sing directly to Lord Von Pragh. She was grateful that the unknown femme fatale was noticeably absent. Knowing that Fiona was jealous of her, it caused a certain triumph within him. He seemed lost in the glory and wonder of the strains of the dying Mimi.

Wasn't it enough that Fiona had to deal with Christiana, who had been quiet for some time? Why the transformation? she questioned. Would there be another outburst from Christiana? Time would tell. Maybe she was at peace with the fact that the mayor of Limerick was interested in Fiona. He obviously was dogged in his pursuit of her. His motives were highly questionable. What cared Christiana as long as she had Lord Von Pragh to herself and nobody else?

At the completion of the performance, Fiona went backstage and entered the area outside where enthusiastic fans grasped and groped for her autograph. Many well-wishers shook her hand, but uppermost in her mind was going to a dive of his Cambridge days and dancing with Lord Von Pragh. Apparently he had been a wild man then, but time and circumstance had abated his modus operandi.

"You don't have to dress up for this joint," Lord Von Pragh said. "Nobody will notice us. Everybody does their own thing here."

Hardly able to contain her excitement, Fiona walked hand in hand to the limousine.

Arriving at a small stone building in an alley, Lord Von Pragh said, "Give me your money."

"What for?" she asked, puzzlement in Fiona's face.

"There may be pickpockets here. I told you it is frequented by intellectuals, artists, aspiring singers, sailors, gamblers, and a sprinkling of pickpockets, which they try to weed out at the door."

"Oh! This is exciting. Here's my money. Put it in your inside pocket."

She smiled a radiant smile as they squeezed into a low-ceilinged dimly lit club. They went downstairs slowly with Lord Von Pragh stepping carefully with his cane. It was a darkened basement drum thumping place with people dancing and smooching so close to one another that Fiona thought it was the most avant-garde place she had ever visited. Pressing against bodies everywhere and with the semi-darkness, it evoked a sense of intimacy. Fiona clung to Lord Von Pragh till they reached the bar. He squeezed her hand reassuringly, sending tingles of excitement through her body.

Nubile women were scantily dressed, revealing outward sexuality. Some men were in casual attire, while others were expensively dressed. There were long-haired bearded artistic types buying drinks for the ladies. Some students pooled their money for a more expensive drink for the piano player who scoffed at those who drank beer or cheap wine.

Lord Von Pragh opted for Chardonnay and a Merlot wine for Fiona and himself. Many foreigners were present, speaking different languages. A towering, handsome fat black crooner sang a wildly romantic song, sending partners to the middle of the floor, kissing and hugging and barely able to move due to the overcrowded condition. Fiona and Lord Von Pragh sipped their wine, almost intoxicated by the cigarette and pipe smoke and hypnotic music.

They got up to dance, barely able to join the body-hugging partners. Putting his hand protectively round her back, Lord Von Pragh drew her to him. She loved the aroma of cedar emanating from his neck and clothing. He kissed her lightly on the neck, sending shivers of delight down her back as she pressed her body to him. She could feel every muscle and sinew of his body, making her feel at one with him. Feeling his penis, strong and erect, she moved closer to him squeezing her thighs tightly round him and moving in rhythm with the romantic music.

"That feels good," he whispered, and he pulled her buttocks to him.

"Kiss your chick," the crooner urged at the conclusion of the song.

Fiona thrust her tongue inside his mouth till she felt consumed by Lord Von Pragh. He was like opium to her revitalized body and soul. Heavenly thoughts about him whirred in her head. This was absolute bliss, she told herself. He evoked such tenderness in her that she was afraid to succumb to her feelings.

"Let's go outside for a breath of fresh air," he said, leading the way to a small courtyard.

There it was, wall to wall, people handing around a joint of cannabis.

"It's been a while since I smoked this," Lord Von Pragh said.

A young ponytailed fellow handed him the joint. He inhaled slowly and deeply three times.

"Now it's your turn, Fiona."

Seeing the relaxed, smiling face of her partner, Fiona inhaled twice.

"Not bad," she said, leaning heavily on Lord Von Pragh. "But I feel a little dizzy."

She passed the joint to a slightly intoxicated blonde next to her who could not wait to get a whiff of the joint.

"There's nothing like good sex and a joint," she confessed. "Do you agree?" she added, addressing Lord Von Pragh. "I come here to get my mojo on."

Lord Von Pragh put his strong arm lovingly round Fiona's shoulder.

"Fiona is my mojo." He winked.

Incensed at the remark, Fiona led the way back to the dance floor. They kissed with such fervor and passion that convinced Fiona that what he said was true. Why had this pot smoker aroused such jealousy within her? She was well aware that her partner loved the attention, and realized that the possessiveness that reared its head was all the more endearing to him.

The club was stifling hot with people flocking down the narrow staircase to join the dancers.

Lord Von Pragh said, "I can't take this heat any longer. Let's go home and make wild passionate love."

The idea thrilled Fiona as she led the way back up to the exit. What a relief it was to breathe the raw, cold drizzly air. However, after a few minutes, they flung their warm coats and scarves around them. Feeling no pain, they hailed a taxi to Fiona's flat. Dubois greeted them with a wagging tail, licking and jumping all over them. Sauntering hand in hand, they took Dubois for a walk. Reluctant to stay outside too long, the dog led the way back to the flat.

Dubois was in an excited mood. Fiona undressed Lord Von Pragh slowly in between kisses, and he slumped down on the bed. After she had undressed herself, Fiona lay beside him. Hyperexcitable Dubois jumped in between them.

"I feel like making mad, passionate love," Lord von Pragh whispered. "You drove me wild with desire all night."

He kissed her tenderly on the cheek, moving closer to her. Fiona felt a trembling of her heart and knew she was in the mood. Dubois stayed irresolutely between them, jumping at the slightest crush to his small anatomy. Fiona pushed him down to the Persian-carpeted floor, but he was up on the bed in a few seconds. He kissed Fiona and Lord Von Pragh and repositioned himself in the middle of them.

"This is not going to work," Lord Von Pragh sighed. "Put him in another room."

Fiona obliged by closing the parlor door on Dubois. The latter barked incessantly a loud piercing cry, which at this time of the morning was bound to disturb the neighbors. He scratched at the door that Fiona thought a tenant would soon be ringing her doorbell. With no choice, she had to allow him back to the bed.

Yes. The dog was truly a man's best friend and would not tolerate anyone coming between the two would-be lovers. Had it been a good idea to take in Dubois for protection? Not that he disliked Lord Von Pragh. Maybe he was in a playful mood. In her scantily low-cut pink nightgown with embroidered lace, Fiona got up and fed him some food.

Dubois ate it voraciously, but no, he had chosen the bed as his resting place. He was not going to insult either of them. Before long, Fiona heard Lord Von Pragh snoring. Damn it! she thought. This had been her golden opportunity to make love with such tenderness such as she had never done before. Totally relaxed and feeling supersexy with the residual effect of the cannabis, she was about to miss this once-in-a-lifetime opportunity. What could this mean?

Was Christiana present wherever Lord Von Pragh decided to rest his head? Apparently so. Nevertheless, Fiona had no proof, and she must give Christiana the benefit of the doubt. Could Christiana be cunning and manipulating the movements of Fiona?

It was certainly within the realm of possibility. However, Fiona trusted her intuition. She slid her hand across his abdomen, but there was no stirring. He was fast asleep, another triumph for Christiana and a missed opportunity for Fiona. How the latter yearned for tumultuous lovemaking. This chance would not pass this way again. Or would it?

Maybe Lord Von Pragh would awaken in the early hours of the morning, when his testosterone level was at its highest, insisting or requesting that they make love. But Fiona was not a morning person. Morning light hurt her eyes, and basically, she considered herself a night person. Was the spirit of Christiana all-encompassing? Maybe a disgruntled spirit had no peace. Perhaps she had less peace in Bedford Castle without the nightly visits of Lord Von Pragh. Why? Oh why couldn't she be at rest?

Fiona had no solution. She was not going to wish animosity or hatred for her but bless her tumultuous lifestyle. Pity was what she needed more than anything else. Christiana had passed into the other world before her time and therefore resented it.

Fiona could have been in her shoes. But she was not. Lord Von Pragh had continued with his life bogged down with a severe limitation of psychic agnosia. But he had been relatively successful considering the current circumstances. Was it his belief in psychic phenomena that pushed him forward? He had to believe in something other than earthly powers when psychic agnosia occurred. Maybe God had been kind to him as he often is when trials beyond human endurance beset a person.

With Dubois curled up between Fiona and Lord Von Pragh, she had no choice but to sleep. In fact, sleep came easily with the combination of wine, cannabis, and Dubois resting protectively against her legs. If only she were married to Lord Von Pragh. No doubt she would pamper him like a spoiled brat who needed love and affection and the assurance that life would not throw another mishap in his direction.

It was time that respite should occur. But there was no telling what Rory McCormack had on his mind. For a politician who had ambition beyond his wildest dreams, he would resort to anything to accomplish that end.

However, Fiona was not of like mind. How she yearned to help the less fortunate, which was also the ambition of Lord Von Pragh. She must demonstrate that she would be his ally and strength in times of duress. What could be more trying than to be deprived of the essential sense of sight?

While Fiona was in a semitrance state, she gave Lord Von Pragh an absent healing of which he was not aware. Time and time again she visualized him being healed by a force that was not of this earthly world. Was it simply a figment of her imagination, or was it actual reality? Reality, she reminded herself, was not necessarily imagination. She called on her grandmother to explain but was not able to decipher what she was telling her. No doubt she approved of the alliance of Lord Von Pragh, but the decision ended there.

At no point did Fiona want to pester her grandmother, but she would have been grateful for an inkling of a successful outcome. How was she to attain this? If she told the average person that she communicated with her grandmother, she knew she would be scoffed at. But this was Fiona's world communicating with a good spirit who would elevate her to a higher realm.

It was not the average person's belief, but something special between Lord Von Pragh and Fiona. They were in tandem about the spirit world, although he was more reticent about it. And why not? He had more to lose by admitting his beliefs than Fiona. He had to present himself as a straight laced politician who would undoubtedly be booted from the House of Parliament if news of this nature were leaked to the press.

Nonetheless, Fiona believed in Lord Von Pragh and wished she could make mad, passionate love to him. They would rise to the same heights of physicality and spirituality and liberate themselves. They were two souls seeking a higher form that could not be explained.

After all, many artists had enjoyed significant achievements by keeping mute about it. It was so satisfying to hear Lord Von Pragh divulge material that heretofore he had not discussed with anyone. Fiona felt liberated by the discussions they shared. She was not some simpleton who believed only what can be proved.

Of this Fiona was certain. Rory McCormack was a devious man intent on getting his way by any means necessary. However, Fiona was single-minded in her pursuit of Lord Von Pragh. What did she now about Rory McCormack other than that he was a big gambler who would tell constituents anything they wanted to believe?

Not so Lord Von Pragh. Somewhat of a loner, he selected his friends carefully, and when they reneged during the crisis, he stayed alone. Music was his soul, ready to distract him at any time. Ever ready to help the less fortunate, he worked towards that direction without guarantee of future success.

CHAPTER 19

"Keep this date open. It is a very important day. I have undertaken to help you. My lawyers, in association with your lawyer, seriously doubt the authenticity of the alleged sister who claims half of your inheritance. Therefore, they have been working tirelessly since you returned from Ireland to prove that Georgina is not your sister. I sincerely hope that you don't mind the interference of my lawyer."

"Not at all," replied Fiona. "In fact, I was going to broach the subject but decided against it, considering your own problems."

"Your problems are mine, Fiona. I don't want to see you gypped out of your father's inheritance, and that means all of it."

"How could I ask for a better friend than you?"

"I hope I mean more to you than that. As I told you before, I want you to be my wife."

"You are really serious."

"Would I take it upon myself to interfere in your affairs if I did not have your best interest at heart?"

"I suppose not."

"Our lawyers feel that Georgina is a sham with no relation whatsoever to you."

"Strangely enough, I felt that way right from the beginning when I met her in Thomas Dwyer's law office. But then I knew very little about my father's private affairs and could scarcely argue about Georgina."

"The lawyers are going into an intensive investigation, which will leave no doubt in the end that you are the sole heir to your father's estate. It'll take time as she has moved frequently and in shady circumstance. But my lawyers have ways and means of getting at the truth."

"When will I know?'

"We are meeting with them and your London lawyer next week. Forgive me for prying into your business. You bring out the macho instinct in me because you are so very much alone in the world."

"You are the only man I need now and forever. I will do anything for you in consideration of your kindness to me."

"And you, my dear, have soared my spirit to unearthly realms when I was sad and depressed. If truth be told, I was in the depths of despair. You didn't know that. The tolling of the bell in a nearby church was my only companion while I sat night after night in Bedford Castle."

"I'll tell you honestly you intimidated me. I thought no man is so sorrowful that his mood cannot be lifted by a kind word."

"When you spoke, I detected a white aura enveloping you. You know that we are meant for each other."

"Yes. I do."

"It was when you decided to set off for London alone that brought about a metamorphosis in me. I resolved to start living again instead of being a recluse who alienated friends."

"I'm glad I did."

"No happier than I am."

"Let's see if we can wind up the saga with the lawyers. We have two wily detectives working on this situation too."

Fiona moved closer to Lord Von Pragh. Assessing her with admiration, he drew her closely to him, kissing her with such a ferocity that stunned her. She reciprocated in kind, and reeling with ecstasy, she fell back in the chair, exultant and exhausted.

"I'll meet you at my flat at twelve noon. Dress warmly," he said.

Lord Von Pragh retreated outdoors, his footsteps treading cautiously in the rising dew and enveloping mist. Arriving at his flat at the designated time, Fiona and Lord Von Pragh were driven by the driver as far as allowed by the police and then sallied forth on foot to Marble Arch. Despite the threatening weather, it seemed the crowd was bigger than previously. The poll tax seemed to be on the minds of the angry protestors, not only because it seemed unreasonable. but in addition the price of food had skyrocketed due to a severe summer drought. Demonstrators' minds were made up that conditions like this could not and would not be tolerated much longer.

Placards and signs swayed as the people pushed towards the shopping center of Oxford Street. Police were in no mood for this turn of events. Lord Von Pragh and Fiona clung to each other as a random crowd pushed past them.

Christmas carols rang out in a nearby block. Shoppers were busy carrying their bags of recently purchased goods and others fending their way into the brightly lit inviting stores. Intent on their purpose. the demonstrators blocked the entrance to stores. The police struggled to move them along, when a group of youngsters and teenagers barged into a store with teddy bears and beautiful toys on display.

A young ragamuffin grabbed the outstretched arms of a fuzzy teddy bear, sending shouts of indignation from the sales staff for the presence of more police to restore law and order. Clutching the cuddly teddy bear to his bosom, several children followed suit and grabbed toys, fleeing on foot to the doorway.

A no-nonsense burly policeman with a gruff look on his face clunked the bear-hugging skinny boy with a nightstick with such force that knocked him out cold to the floor. Fiona saw him turn deathly pale and blood streaming from his head down to his innocent face onto the teddy bear. Tempers boiled, and outrage ensued with women and men throwing fists and curses at the policeman.

Suddenly there was a blast of sirens, with horns honking and lights flashing. Ambulances screeched to a halt outside the store. Fists were clenched in mounting anger, making the police cower behind the ambulance crew.

The injured little boy and the teddy bear were placed on a stretcher in an ambulance and sped away to St. Thomas Hospital. Several of the robbers were placed in handcuffs and shoved roughly into police vans. Parents cursed and screamed at the police.

"Robert," Fiona said, "you've got to help these children. It's Christmastime, and they probably receive no presents because their parents are too poor. These are the forgotten, the lonely, the children who cry on Christmas Day instead of sharing laughter and joy. There are too many of them. What does the government care about them?"

"Let me see what I can do to help the poor, misfortunate buggers," he said.

"This is what happens when children have to go to bed hungry, and then they have the audacity to try to introduce the poll tax," Lord Von Pragh confided to a television reporter.

"Let's go to the Old Bailey and help them," said the journalist. "Let's see that they get fair treatment on Christmas week."

Police reinforcements were arriving quickly and urgently. Fiona and Lord Von Pragh joined the journalist and photographer in the car. At the courthouse, the magistrate sitting sternly in a big chair in front of a square table on which rested a gavel ordered each frightened child brought before him. Bail was set at twenty pounds each plus restitution for the price of the toy they had stolen. Mothers and fathers were incensed at the high bail, taking into consideration it was Christmas week.

Suddenly Fiona stepped forward.

"Your honor," she said, "Lord Von Pragh here would like to pay bail for each of these poor children who are hard hit at the worst of times. These are children who never receive a Christmas gift, and they availed themselves of the opportunity. Given these circumstances, Lord Von Pragh would like to pay bail and the amount it costs for the gift, which he knows they stole."

"I don't like to remand anyone to jail or juvenile detention center at this time of year," the magistrate said in a kindly voice, "but if Lord Von Pragh wishes to pay, the charges will be dismissed on condition that this is the first offense of each child."

The children looked with imploring but nonetheless happy eyes at Lord Von Pragh.

"They are grateful," whispered Fiona.

Hearts full of longing for a good supper and gratitude to their benefactor, they glanced at Lord Von Pragh and Fiona. The latter smiled sweetly towards them.

"Let it not be said," the magistrate intoned, "that there are still kind people on this earth. Don't think that luck will always be on your side. All of you could have spent time in jail. It is not a pretty picture in jail as anybody who has been incarcerated can tell you." He glanced sternly from one thief to the other.

The magistrate nodded approvingly at Lord Von Pragh and Fiona, bidding them good evening and a merry Christmas.

Outside the Old Bailey, Lord Von Pragh said, "Let's find out about the young boy who was rushed to the hospital." The young thieves and their parents surrounded Lord Von Pragh and Fiona, offering their thanks.

"You can thank me better by saying a little prayer for me. It will truly be appreciated."

"Ay! Ay!" they rejoined.

Approaching the ambulance, which was waiting outside, Lord Von Pragh addressed the driver. "Tell me the condition of the young boy who was hit on the head. You know the one. He was hugging a blood-spattered stolen teddy bear."

"That wee bloke I hope will be all right. He was knocked unconscious."

"May I see him?"

"No. He's still unconscious. He'll probably have a bad headache when he awakens. Between the three of us, the bobby was wrong to wallop him on the head."

"I agree." Lord Von Pragh and Fiona nodded.

"The poor always get the short end of the stick," said the ambulance driver.

"We'll visit him tomorrow and get him a nice red fire engine, which will keep him occupied," Fiona said.

Walking through the mist, which turned to torrential rain, they hailed a taxi, which brought them to Lord Von Pragh's residence.

As they sipped a glass of wine, they switched on the news.

"The poll tax," the announcer said, "does not stand much of a chance of being passed in the House of Parliament. Such an outcry from the citizens of London will make it impossible. Mayhem was let loose on Oxford Street when scores of young hooligans looted stores at the height of the shopping season, verifying what we always knew. Children go to bed hungry, and they've resorted to taking the law into their own hands. A five-year-old boy is unconscious in St. Thomas Hospital after he was walloped on the head by a policeman. Parliament had better veto the proposed poll tax before people are killed in the demonstrations. An unidentified male paid the bail for sixty people at the Old Bailey."

Back at her own flat, the lamentations of the wind creaked throughout the cornices and crevices, causing Fiona to feel ill at ease. Whether Dubois was sensing her psyche, but he seemed distinctly nervous, retreating under the couch with his nose peeping out. To drown out the lamentations, Fiona turned opera on the radio. *That's better,* she thought. It distracted her somewhat, but not nearly enough that she should feel more relaxed. When the phone rang, she jumped, feeling her arm twitch as she picked it up.

It was Lord Von Pragh, which made her heart thrill with delight and ease the tension that had seemed to envelop her.

"Fiona, my darling," he said, "I hope Dubois is taking good care of you."

"The little bugger is hiding under the armchair. I think he's afraid of alternate bouts of howling of the wind and the rattling of the window panes."

"I have good news for you. I know you are scheduled to be at the Royal Opera House tomorrow evening. Let's meet at the mews, and from there, we'll head to my lawyer's office."

Exultant at this news, Fiona reminded Lord Von Pragh that she missed him very much and would be delighted to see him tomorrow be it fair weather or foul. It was relatively early in the evening, and considering the hectic day ahead, she decided to go to bed early. Despite the good news she had received from Lord Von Pragh that night, her dreams were beset by nightmarish events. She could hardly recall on awakening what the nightmare was about. In fact, she felt it simply lucky that she couldn't remember what had transpired. It was a mishmash of horrible events.

Nevertheless, looking her loveliest, Fiona arrived at Lord Von Pragh's penthouse. Together and feeling loved beyond words, they rode in his car to the lawyer's office. The premises were situated in the most fashionable area of Kensington, which Fiona was convinced only the crème de la crème could afford. They entered the law office of Wrigglesworth and Gillette, Esq. Antique clocks resting on the mantelpiece and lining the walls ticked and tocked the eleven o'clock hour.

"I'm delighted to meet you, Ms. Morgan. I'm Charles Wrigglesworth, who has represented the Von Praghs for many years. I won't tell you how many. You'd think I'm old."

They shook hands, and he introduced Mr. Gillette. Mr. Wrigglesworth said, "Please be seated and make yourselves comfortable.

They seated themselves on comfortable leather chairs divided by a table.

"We have all the facts," said Mr. Wrigglesworth, "which are quite muddlesome even to me. And I've heard it all over the years. It's something of international intrigue. To begin with, your father had married six times. All his wives were American born. Not one of them was Irish. This Georgina was born into a poverty-stricken Irish family of eight, all of whom were illegitimate. Naturally, they scattered in different directions at an early age to escape the squalor and poverty to which they were destined. Here we are only interested in Georgina."

Mr. Wrigglesworth cleared his throat before continuing.

"With no education, Georgina went to England, where she worked as a housekeeper to a very wealthy gentleman who had many secrets in his closet. But he trusted Georgina and was very good to her financially, which she had not known before. She severed all connections with her family except for one sister who still lives in a one-room cottage where she was born.

With the money she had accumulated, Georgina started moving in better circles. At one such party, she met the politician Rory McCormack, who took a real fancy to her. He liked her aggressive ways. Eventually she confided to him that she had not been happy within herself being a female, and she wanted to go to Amsterdam for a sex change operation. Unstable at that time from taking daily doses of hormones, she persuaded Mr. McCormack to finance her operation. Already smitten by Georgina—and believe me, from what I hear, she was possessed of a very magnetic and persuasive personality—he vowed to help her when he could.

His only means of getting ahead financially was through politics, and he used this to introduce her to the Irish gentry who had no living heirs. Between both of them, they wiggled and waggled money here and there, with Rory McCormack the instigator. He paid the down payment on a certain portion of the transgender operation. When Georgina realized that he could no longer foot the bill for the operation, she left him. Desperate to continue the relationship, he promised to get the money from any source. And the source is you, Fiona."

Looking her squarely in the eyes, Mr. Wrigglesworth resumed, "Rory McCormack and Georgina concocted the story that the latter was conceived by the nurse and Mr. Frederick Morgan. The nurse has been interviewed several times by me personally and vows that only you, Fiona, was born to her. Even at the time of her pregnancy, she was already engaged to her boyfriend, who was in financial difficulties. But he gave his permission, and the nurse was paid what was then an exorbitant amount of money by Mr. Frederick Morgan. That is the sum total of Georgina, who had no claim to your father's estate."

Mr. Wrigglesworth opened a bulging folder and said, "In fact, your mother's husband testifies under oath to that effect. In other words, Georgina needs a large sum of money to complete the transgender operation plus hotel, transportation expenses, and other incidentals to Denmark. Poor Rory McCormack could not, under any circumstances, foot the bill of such magnitude to keep her happy."

"What's to be done about it?" enquired Fiona.

"The two fraudsters have the choice to contest it. The alternative is to have your real mother, with her husband, deny the fact that Georgina is in no way connected to you. Never has been and never will be. They have asked us to settle three times. There is no settlement to be made. You and you alone is the sole heir to your beloved father's estate. The law deals very harshly with those who would defy the law."

"I care not one iota about what my father left me," Fiona said timidly. "He was a wonderful father, even though I didn't see him as often as I would have liked. I felt lonely, but the times I was with him, I wish they would have been prolonged forever."

"To get down to brass facts," Mr. Wrigglesworth added, "you are not going to foot the money for Georgina's operations, which can continue for years and for which Rory McCormack has no means to support her. Between his gambling debts and drinking habits, I can hardly fathom how he can support himself. He likes to live high on the hog, but where the money comes from baffles me. God knows what he'll resort to one day with these mounting bills."

Fiona gasped a sigh of relief.

Lord Von Pragh clutched her hand reassuringly and said, "Fiona has to go now for singing practice and then the performance at the Royal Opera House this evening. We have no time to spare."

The air was raw and cold, save for areas where flits of sunlight shone. The driver was thankfully at their disposal and drove them to Lord Von Pragh's penthouse. The housekeeper had prepared a delicious meal of fresh salmon with goat cheese, cucumber, and slices of whole wheat bread, which they ate ravenously. She also packed a steak bone for Dubois.

"I don't know what it is," Lord Von Pragh said, "but my mind seems to be working overtime. For some reason, I fear for your safety. You are so alone, and this awful situation with the mayor of Limerick had to rear its ugly head."

"Peculiar as it may sound, I've had bad vibes too. I can't pinpoint it, but I've a distinct feeling of ill ease these days."

"You have Dubois. He'll alert you to anything, and besides, you have the stone I gave you from Egypt."

"I hope I don't get confused and mislay the stone. Oh! I just don't feel myself. I don't know what it is."

Fiona glanced nervously from side to side and behind her. Reaching out her hand, she grabbed Lord Von Pragh to her and entwined his arm in hers.

"This is ridiculous." She laughed nervously. "I didn't tell you about the wonderful dream I had when I stayed that night at Bedford Castle. It wasn't exactly a dream. It was more of a vision, if you believe in visions."

"Why? Of course, I do."

"My grandmother appeared in the dream in a beautiful diaphanous gown and advised me to go to London. She said that certain countries are unlucky for people and others are lucky. She specifically advised me to go to London. I'm not going to tell you all the dream."

"Did she mention me?"

"Not precisely. But she told me I would find fame and fortune and true love."

"That's me as far as true love is concerned. Did she tell you I would be flawed by visual agnosia?"

"Not a word about that. In my eyes, you are the perfect person."

"That's what Christiana believed too. That's why she had such a hard time letting me go even in death." Lord Von Pragh reached over and kissed her with such tenderness that it almost melted her away. She was lost in the wonder and glory of his kiss.

Snuggling up to her, he said, "I'm glad you changed the subject. I was afraid of your state of mind with wild imaginings of dire forebodings. Be on your way with the driver, and I'll see you at the Royal Opera House this evening. I never tire of your rendition of the dying Mimi."

Fiona passed a beautiful semicircle of rainbow decked in blue, yellow, and a touch of red hues. When she arrived at her flat, Dubois gushed over her at the smell of the steak bone. She unwrapped it and gave it to him. He was so preoccupied with it that he refused to leave it in the flat and went outside, dangling the bone between his teeth.

CHAPTER 20

That night, when Fiona appeared on stage, she immediately recognized the femme fatale sitting beside Lord Von Pragh. When he had confessed his undying love for Fiona, why was he accompanied by a woman who could arouse the envy of any London woman? Trying to ignore it, Fiona gave a moving performance of Mimi, pouring her heart and soul into it. Lord Von Pragh's eyes seemed to be glued to Fiona while occasionally whispering in the ear and smiling pleasantly at the femme fatale.

Perplexing to Fiona was who this woman was. She was a natural beauty who could sweep the most urbane man off his feet. To add insult to injury, a man who appeared to be a foreigner was also commanding her attention. Why oh why must some woman have all the luck? Fiona wondered. Yet beautiful women weren't always lucky, surmised Fiona. There were the unwanted suitors like Rory McCormack and the near-nigh impossibles like Lord Von Pragh, the latter who had a deceased wife who clung tenaciously to him and interfered in his relationship with Fiona.

However, Christiana had lain low in the last few weeks for what reason was incomprehensible. Even though Fiona desired Lord Von Pragh more than life itself, he seemed to have cooled off. Yet in other ways, he had not. He was out to protect her from every angle, for which she was seriously indebted to him.

What if Lord Von Pragh fell in love with this femme fatale? Men and women have been known to change their minds without much notice, something which caused Fiona a considerable amount of concern. At her last bow, Lord Von Pragh and the foreigner threw a huge bouquet of flowers on stage. Fiona bowed graciously again and wondered who the couple was, who seemed to be friends of Lord Von Pragh.

"Come to my dressing room later," Fiona said.

True to their word, they did. After dipping champagne, they set off for the exclusive Stork Club. Fiona was miffed that she knew very little about the femme fatale.

Quite boldly, she enquired, "Who is this exquisite lady and her friend?"

"I thought I would keep you guessing," Lord Von Pragh said. "May I introduce you to Senor Marco DeBlanco and his wife of many years."

This puzzled Fiona. Surprisingly she said, "I'm so jealous of you. I don't want to be, but I've seen you in the company of my boyfriend so many times. I thought you were a twosome"

"Not at all," said Marco. "Robert and I attended boarding school together in Gordonstoun in Scotland, where we had to take cold showers every morning, and then Cambridge University, where it was a little better off. Robert was the best man at our wedding. Unfortunately, due to my job in the diplomatic corp., I have to travel extensively, and he keeps my wife from getting lonely during my long absences."

Fiona smiled and instantly warmed up to both of them.

"Robert and I are old school chums," Marco continued. "For old time's sake and to reassure your pretty spiritual girlfriend, who looks like she descended from heaven, let's go to one of our old haunts. I don't want to gamble tonight, but I'll watch the goings-on."

Marco confided to Fiona that Lord Von Pragh had been one of the best boxers at Cambridge University.

"I never saw that side of him," Fiona said.

"No. He's very gentle with women. That's why they fall hook, line, and sinker for him. It's gotten him into trouble many times. I don't know whether you've heard, but one woman committed suicide, which dragged his name into the mud."

"Yes. He has told me about it." Fiona thought to herself that she hoped she would not be the next victim. "Lord Von Pragh has been nothing but a gentleman to me," Fiona said.

"She knows I would do anything for her," Lord Von Pragh said.

The conversation revolved around their youthful escapades in which Fiona learned a lot about Lord Von Pragh. After imbibing more champagne, they dropped off Fiona at her flat. But not before seeing her inside the door. The wonder and glory of his kisses sent waves of rapture through her body. He was becoming more sensitive and caring than he had ever been before. No doubt Fiona appreciated that immeasurably.

While savoring Lord Von Pragh's kisses and feeling on top of the world, a kaleidoscope of brilliant white lights were twirling and dancing on the walls of the sitting room. It seemed never–ending, and Fiona luxuriated in what she could not decipher. What did this mean? It could only herald good tidings. Was this a product of her imagination, or something to be realized in time to come? Her eyes glanced furtively round the room. The twirling and dancing of these nonearthly lights continued. It stirred a very comforting feeling in her. But she was not sure what it meant. It could only mean a pleasurable experience.

However, Fiona's hopes were high that she concluded that everything would be all right. Was she capable of differentiating between good and bad? Absolutely. She was clairvoyant, clairaudient, and clairsentient. So was Lord Von Pragh. Somehow she understood that the twirling white lights had some association with Lord Von Pragh. If only she could pinpoint the connection. Maybe it was not meant to be for now. Did the future hold the key?

CHAPTER 21

It was a whispering, windless, moonless night. All was still within and without, save for Dubois crunching on his steak bone. Lone footsteps echoed in an unknown quarter of the building. For some unfathomable reason, Fiona felt a distinct sense of unease. Her heart skipped a beat. Why this state of events? she wondered.

Several minutes later, as Fiona was thinking of Robert with a heart full of longing, her musings were interrupted by a sudden knock on the door. Dubois ceased munching on his bone and let out a menacing growl. Oh! How consumed with joy she would be if he should appear in the flesh. Then there was another knock.

"Fire. Fire. Fire. Evacuate!" a voice, rough and gruff, said with a loud thud on the door.

Without further ado, Fiona opened the door. Eyes aglow with a look of mockery, Rory McCormack barged in. Sweat pouring from his corpulent body and reeking of alcohol, he grabbed Fiona. She let out a gasp. Her heart beat with a fury she could not control. He closed the door with a grim look of satisfaction. Dubois stood back and bared his teeth. Low, menacing growls emanated from his throat. He bit Rory on the leg with such a ferocity that blood seeped down through his ragged pants and the purple carpet. He let out a snarl and kicked the dog with such a fury that it obviously pained Dubois. The latter retreated with a limp, licking his body.

"Aha! I got you!" Rory exclaimed.

Fiona recoiled in horror as Rory lunged toward her. He ripped off the bodice of her nightgown, making her feel sensitive and vulnerable. She kicked with all her might and main. He seemed oblivious to it. He threw her to the couch, banging her head with such force against the stone wall that she suspected she might have fractured her skull.

"Now," he said, "you don't think I'm good enough for you," his voice dripping with sarcasm.

She wanted to run to the bedroom to grasp the Egyptian stone Robert had given her. Temporarily she was oblivious to what was happening to her. Slipping in and out of consciousness, she was aware that her legs were wide apart and her ankles fastened by a strong garment. She was totally naked. Her hands were bound as Rory heaved toward her. He slapped her across the face till she was almost blinded by the vicious slaps. With a knife at her throat his erect penis was trying to penetrate her.

"Our child shall be entitled to your inheritance," he said with conviction in his voice.

Fiona squirmed and flailed and kicked.

"Please help me," was her silent invocation to her grandmother.

She visualized Robert, sending a message to him that she was in dire need. However, she dismissed that as hopeless. What could a blind man with visual agnosia do to help her? Raising his fist, Rory punched Fiona in the face and nose. She was unaware how many times.

"I'll disfigure you," he muttered, "so that no man will want you, you cunning bitch." The blade of the shiny, jagged knife was at her jugular vein.

"No! No!" she cried, twisting her head away.

Was it her imagination? she wondered. Fiona thought she heard a noise, which exacerbated her headache. Dubois let out several weak yelps and one loud one.

"He-help . . . help," Fiona stammered weakly.

Fiona's voice trailed off. Words would not come. She thought she had a glimmering of the figure of Lord Von Pragh. Incapable of thinking straight, she banished that idea. Confused, sore, and hurt, she lay motionless. She heard a commotion outside in the hallway.

A loud series of raps on the door ensued. Suddenly a force mightier than the mightiest wind struck the door once and then twice. Dubois leapt to his feet and fell down. Rory McCormack held the knife in his hand. Fiona could hardly believe her luck. It was Robert who threw the knife out of the hand of Rory. The latter went to retrieve it. Dubois leapt on him, biting his hand several times. Robert hit him with such a mighty blow of his cane that sent Rory reeling.

There was something different about Robert. He seemed to be radiating with a white glow around his face. His eyes dazzled like stars in the moonlight. Rory staggered up from the floor. Robert hit him again and again with his cane and his fists. Rory was out cold.

"No, my love, you gave me what no physician could give me. I searched for my eyesight to be restored for two years all over the world. Now it's back. I can see every contour of your exquisite face, eyes, and body." Tears welling in his eyes, making him more aristocratic and appealing, he kissed her gently, making sure that he would not hurt her.

"Police!" a voice shouted from outside the door. Lord Von Pragh let three policemen in. A blonde helmeted policeman fetched a multicolored counterpane from the bedroom and covered Fiona with it. He unfastened her ankles.

The other policemen said, "Lord Mayor McCormack, you are under arrest for breaking and entering this flat, attempted murder with a deadly weapon, attempted rape, stealing money from constituents, cruelty to an animal."

Rory McCormack staggered to his knees.

The policeman added, "There may be other serious charges pending. You have the right to remain silent. Anything you say will be held against you in a court of law. Turn around. Put your hands behind your back."

Rory took a leap forward and flung open the window. He jumped on the windowsill. The policeman pulled him off. The hulking Rory was placed in handcuffs and escorted to a black maria.

"Now that these negative vibes are behind you, let's get treatment for you and Dubois," Lord Von Pragh said.

Hearing his name mentioned, the Jack Russell terrier leapt on Fiona's chest, kissing her.

"It's my turn," Lord Von Pragh said. "You've given me the most precious gift of sight. I thought I would not be able to reach you on time. The odds were against me. Christiana tried desperately to pull me back into the penthouse. The door wouldn't open downstairs."

Christiana kept whispering, "You'll die in a crash. I decided to defy her. I think it was the only time I have. There came a moment when I decided you needed help more. I jumped into the car. Suddenly a purple orb appeared before my eyes and a white seraphic light at my feet. I could see a little. But as I drove like an insane man, I could see as clearly as I did two years ago. Nothing short of a miracle happened."

With tears streaming down his cheeks, he clutched Fiona, kissing her. A lump arose in her throat so that she was unable to speak.

ABOUT THE AUTHOR

Teresa Ryan was born in County Tipperary in Ireland. Although a native of Ireland, she graduated as a registered nurse from England. She has been living in the USA for several years. Her foremost interest is writing, but she makes her living by working in the field of drug and alcohol rehabilitation and occupational health. Besides writing, Teresa is also interested in the paranormal.

CPSIA information can be obtained
at www.ICGtesting.com
Printed in the USA
LVOW03s0028150817
544949LV00002B/265/P